# CARVED IN STONE

## FAMILY STONE #2 CONNOR

## LISA HUGHEY

December 2013

Lisa Hughey

ISBN: 978-0-9840428-7-6

Print ISBN: 978-0-9991951-8-5

 Created with Vellum

# CARVED IN STONE

By Lisa Hughey

*To my family.*

## CHAPTER 1

"Connor!"

Connor Stone's oldest brother, Jack, yelled through the doorway of his office. The sound traveled all the way down the hall and through Con's closed door.

Con yanked his door open and stomped toward the reception area and Jack's office. "Jesus, Jack." He swiped a fall of blond hair from his eyes as he strode past Ava, Jack's assistant. Con steeled himself to greet her casually with a quick smile, an informal wave, keeping his tone and demeanor low-key so that she would have no idea how much he wanted her. "Hey, Ava."

"Hello, Connor," she replied softly as he barged into Jack's office. Peripherally, he noted her conservative, trim red suit and matching fingernails. The lush contours of her smoking hot body were hidden beneath the staid boxy clothes. Not that he should be noticing her body, but hell he was a guy.

He breathed a quick sigh of relief as he successfully managed to make it past her without revealing any of the lust that he felt. She was Jack's assistant and therefore totally off limits. Plus he was pretty sure he made her nervous.

"What the hell is your deal?" Con's suppressed desire made his voice sharper than he intended.

"I need you."

Con tried not to let the words mean too much but he could feel his chest swell and his throat get a little tight. He was still trying to live down his wild, out-of-control teenage past, even though he was twenty-eight years old and had retired from the Army after ten years and multiple tours. "What for?"

"Close the door for a sec."

Con shut the door and raised his blond eyebrows. Jack shifted in his massive desk chair and flattened his lips. He hadn't seen Jack this out of sorts since the day that Jess and Shelley, their half-sister and her mother, had come to live with them at the Stone Mansion twenty years ago. Their bastard of a father, Jackson Stone Senior, told the whole family Jack was the man of the house and promptly left. Jack had been fourteen.

Con stood in front of Jack's desk, military stiff, feet apart, hands clasped behind his back in parade rest.

"At ease, soldier." Jack chuckled. "While I love the fact that you consider me like your commanding Lord and Master—"

Con snorted. His brother always knew how to push it.

"You're out of the Army now," Jack continued. "There's no need for military protocol in the office."

But the military had given him the structure he needed and the discipline to become a better version of himself. Con shrugged. "I'm comfortable with it," he said simply.

Jack's moment of amusement was gone, replaced by a

somber frown. "Okay. I have to be out of the office for a few days. Unfortunately."

"Do you need intel for your trip?"

"No." If anything his frown got deeper. "That part is taken care of."

Jack stared off into the distance, his face a mask of grumpiness and annoyance. He rubbed a hand over his mouth and shook his head to clear whatever had taken root in his mind. Con thought he saw a flash of worry in Jack's eyes but he knew that wasn't right. Nothing scared Jack. He was the ultimate protector, the ultimate big brother, and the head of their family since the age of fourteen. Damn their irresponsible father.

"Muscle?" Con asked with bemusement. That seemed unlikely. Jack could handle anything.

Another smile quirked Jack's mouth. "Pretty sure of yourself, aren't you?"

About some things, yes. About lots of others, not a chance. But he wasn't about to share that with Jack.

"It's a Stone Consulting job," Jack clarified. "Classified."

They'd all had jobs that had been classified at one time or another, except for Ava Sanchez. Jack had hired her straight out of college from Cal State Monterey Bay. She'd been with his brother since the beginning of GHR and Stone Consulting. Con knew that her degree was in global studies with a concentration in nongovernment organizations — not that he'd happened to read her personnel file or anything—and she never quite looked him in the eyes.

"I really need your help on a separate job." Jack stared out the reflective glass window, the view of the Monterey Bay obscured by lingering morning fog. Wisps of clouds drifted lazily in the gray sky.

Connor tried not to let Jack's words raise his hopes. Usually his contribution to the company was relegated to legal hacking, keeping both companies' firewalls intact, and muscle when they needed an extra body on an op. But now, Jack needed his help?

Con stayed silent. He had no idea where Jack was going with this. When Connor just waited patiently, Jack finally said, "You can get so quiet it's freaky. How are we even related?"

And there it was. Connor's reminder that he wasn't like the other Stone siblings. He wasn't the oldest, he wasn't the charmer, he wasn't the sister. Hell, he didn't even look like his brothers and sister. They had dark hair and green or hazel eyes while Con was blond with a really weird mix of brown and gold eyes.

He was the leftover. The extra. His father had reminded him of that fact often enough growing up. When he was a teenager he'd grabbed attention by acting out, being crazy. Fortunately the Army cured him of that habit. Now he had one motto: *Deeds not words*.

Con had to play it calm. *Deeds not words*. He was finally being given the chance to show that he wasn't the same crazy, spoiled boy that Jack heard about after he left home.

"Can you run an intensive background check on José Fernandez?"

"Sure." Connor waited for more information, wondering why that name sounded familiar. "Am I looking for anything specific?"

"I don't know." Jack rubbed his finger along his scarred eyebrow. He'd never confessed how he had scarred it but Con had enough experience in the Army to know that a bullet had come way too close to his brother's brain. Thank God he had a hard fucking head.

"I need anything and everything you can find on the guy. There's got to be something there, even if no one has found it yet. I don't want to influence your search, so I'm keeping it vague. But I believe he is dirty."

Connor's interest was piqued. A puzzle. "You got it. Anything else?"

"Don't tell anyone what you are working on."

Con shrugged. That wouldn't be a problem.

"Stay here a sec." Jack pressed the intercom on his phone. "Ava, my office now."

Con jerked. He tried to avoid being in small enclosed spaces with her. "You want me to leave?" He hoped his tone wasn't as desperate as he was feeling.

For whatever reason, the last few weeks he'd had more trouble than usual avoiding her. And every time he saw her, his heart rate soared and his thoughts went increasingly to pictures of them together. Not that he would ever do anything about those pictures. He had changed, matured, and he wasn't going to destroy his newfound image by getting busy with an employee.

"No. I still need you here."

Ava opened the door and hurried to the office entrance.

"Yes?" She hovered half in, half out of the doorway. Connor cut a quick glance her way but she was completely focused on Jack. She never said much, even though he knew she spoke four different languages. She was efficient, organized, had the proper attitude and mindset for the Global Humanitarian Relief, and probably didn't know everything they did at GHR's subsidiary, Stone Consulting.

"I'm going out of town. And I've got some instructions for you." Jack tapped the blotter on his desk. "And Connor."

Jack waited one more second and then said, "I'm leaving Connor in charge of the office."

"Me?" And damn if Con's voice didn't rise slightly like a prepubescent boy getting asked out by the hottest girl in school.

"Yeah, you," Jack said as if putting Con in charge made perfect sense. "Riley is delivering books and school supplies to Sulu Island in the Philippines. Jess and Colin are in England until next Tuesday getting his stuff ready to move here. I have to go out of town and I want a Stone in charge."

Jack's brow lifted, as if trying to impart some silent message, but Con was too distracted to interpret that look. Con could care less what the message was. This was a huge step.

A fierce sense of pride flooded him. Jack was entrusting GHR, his personal baby, to Con. But he'd take that out and examine it later. Right now he needed to focus on logistics. "How long are you going to be gone?"

"I don't know." Jack continued tapping the pen. "And I don't know what my comm options will be so I may be out of cell reach for some of my trip."

Con wondered at the lack of information. Jack didn't seem to be trying to be intentionally vague. If anything he seemed irritated and out of sorts. Con tilted his head, waiting for more info. But Jack didn't answer his unspoken question.

"Ava, is there anything hot right now?"

"Just the situation with Riley." Her husky voice scraped over Connor's spine like a lover's fingernails over his naked back, and his body responded accordingly. Hell, this was why he tried to avoid her.

"So you're on." Jack pointed at Con. But then he got one last dig in by cautioning, "Don't fuck it up."

Connor's good humor deflated faster than a parachute canopy after a flare.

*Thanks for the vote of confidence, bro.* But he didn't say the words out loud. Couldn't. He'd always be the youngest, no value added, just some leftover kid that ended up living with the Stone family, related by birth but that's it. Sometimes he wondered why he'd ever come to work for Jack.

"And no having sex on my desk, damn Jess and Colin."

Ava flushed a deep red, her face brighter than the fire engine color of her suit. Her dark eyes were wide as she rushed out of the room without saying a word.

"Are you trying to get sued?" Connor burst out. "Why would you say that? I barely know her." And dammit. Is that really what Jack thought of him? That Con would bone Ava on his desk? Hadn't he avoided her for nine long months, keeping his distance because he was making the effort to be responsible? To show Jack he was worthy of the job? To show everyone that he'd changed?

Suddenly, Con couldn't get the vision of Ava, her suit jacket gaped open, skirt rucked up around her waist, her black hair tumbling over her bare breasts and her long, sleek legs wrapped around him as he pounded home.

He'd constantly, for the nine months he'd worked here, tried to think about Ava in a completely non-sexual way. He focused on her efficiency at keeping them organized and on track, her dedication to her job, and her shyness around him.

But that picture of her, red lips plumped and dark eyes bright, sprawled on top of Jack's desk kept shoving its way into his mind. Jesus, was it getting hot in here?

And why could he *not* get that picture out of his head?

AVA SCURRIED toward her desk and cursed her tendency to blush. Luckily, with her swarthy skin tone and her current healthy tan—she'd spent a decent amount of time at the beach this summer—her blush likely wasn't *too* noticeable. However, she couldn't completely hide her deep embarrassment. When Jack had issued his 'no sex on the desk' command, she'd had no chance to temper her reaction. It was as if he'd reached right into her favorite fantasy and blurted it out to Connor.

She sighed. Connor, who never even noticed her.

Oh, he acknowledged her. He smiled. Said hello. But there was distance in their interactions that she was pretty sure was deliberate. And since they had very few interactions, none personal, she knew he didn't want to get to know her.

Maybe on the outside she appeared as a confident, well-dressed, well-groomed woman, but on the inside she was still that painfully shy wallflower, the migrant worker who didn't quite belong, who squeaked when spoken to and couldn't ever act normal in a social situation.

She'd worked hard to overcome her natural reticence. To learn to be polished and to strive for classy and sophisticated. To eradicate the dust and dirt from the fields and her native Sinaloan accent. She'd come a long way in the last eight years, but she still had difficulty speaking to men she found attractive. And she definitely found Connor Stone attractive.

"Sorry, Ava," Jack called from his office. She knew he was. He was gruff and a little rough around the edges, but he meant well. He'd given her a job right out of college and helped her acclimate to a new world with affection and patience. He treated all his employees like family, which meant he frequently didn't think before he spoke.

Jack, she could handle. She grinned. "Expect my lawsuit in the mail," she quipped back, completely at ease with her totally hot boss. And he was. Totally hot. At thirty-four, he was also a little on the old side for her. But Ava wasn't attracted to Jack. He didn't make her girl parts tingle the way his brother did. Jack was like the older brother she'd never had and always wanted.

Jack gave a shout of laughter.

Why had Jack said that? Could he know that she frequently daydreamed about the youngest Stone brother? All the other women in the office were *loco* over Riley. And no doubt Riley was extremely handsome, smooth, and very charming. He always made her feel feminine and special. But he did that to everyone. Ava preferred the quiet confidence and the understated smarts of Connor Stone.

He was physically intimidating, as big as Jack and definitely as muscular. Since she wasn't a simpering, skinny swizzle stick, but a solid woman with more curves than she'd like and the build of a peasant, Ava appreciated Connor's bulk. She imagined that he would make her feel delicate and dainty if he wrapped his massive biceps around her and cupped her ass in his large palms.

"Hey." Connor stood in front of her desk.

Ava jerked and blinked up at him. She could feel an even deeper flush thunder through her body like a wave of heat. Great, while she'd been daydreaming, he'd been watching her imagine him naked and wrapped around her. "Er. Hello."

"Ignore him. He's an idiot."

"Okay. Thanks."

And if only he'd shut up then, because that was the perfect place to stop. Instead, he kept going. "Of course we aren't going to...."

Of course. Because no way could a guy that good looking, that smart, that *everything*, ever want to have sex with her. Ava's temper began to simmer. "Of course not." Her snide tone left no room for interpretation.

Connor looked very uncomfortable as he figured out that he'd just insulted her. "Uh, I don't think that came out the way I meant it."

And like that she boiled over. "How did you mean it?" she said sweetly, softly. She blinked at him with her most innocent, wide-eyed, non-threatening expression and for the first time truly looked him in the eyes. He had gorgeous eyes, a sunburst of caramel, chocolate, and pale green in a kaleidoscope of color. Tawny, gold, predatory.

He was a very smart man. And he'd figured out that no matter what he said, he was trapped and going to offend her. Like the very smart man he was, Connor backed away. "I meant no disrespect."

If that was the way he wanted to leave it. "Fine."

That stereotypical Latina temper was a stereotype for a reason, but she usually left her hothead reactions at the door. She needed this job and most importantly, she wanted this job to atone for the past. It was a bonus that she loved working here. She loved that she was using her degree but also doing some good. GHR was the perfect vehicle for her need to do penance. For her luck in surviving when Maria and the others...hadn't.

"Ava...."

He wasn't going to go away until she forgave him for the insult and let him off the hook. Too bad she didn't want to forgive him.

"Sure. None taken," Ava said dismissively, clearly lying. She purposely stared at her monitor and started going through her email. The box was relatively light before a holiday weekend.

Connor stood in front of her desk, arms hanging limply at his sides, half-turned toward Jack's office, half-facing her, as if undecided about what to do next.

She continued to pretend that she was ultra-busy, praying he would go away so that she could run to the bathroom and compose herself. She could hear Jack on the phone in his office, arranging the company jet to be at the Monterey regional airport. Soon.

Jack didn't sound happy. And she wondered why he was doing his own scheduling rather than having her take care of it. There was plenty of work that he took care of himself already. But he always had her schedule their pilot, Shane, and make the company travel arrangements.

Connor hadn't left the area by her desk and his presence was beginning to make her sweat. She wondered if Connor was going to use Jack's office while Jack was gone, and if so, how was she going to get any work done with him less than twenty feet away and always just...there? She'd be a distracted mess the entire time.

She randomly clicked on an email from a sender she didn't recognize but when she opened it the body was blank. She absently deleted it as she monitored Connor's movements hoping he would go away so she could concentrate.

Out of the corner of her eye, she noted his feet had started moving.

Only he wasn't leaving. He was stalking toward her like a leopard toward its prey. Finally, all she could see was his thick, muscular thighs and the intriguing bulge in his crotch, covered by tan cargo pants, before he slammed his hands down on her desk, his blunt fingers and wide palms flattened on top of her desk.

His biceps rippled as he leaned close, his broad torso loomed over her and Ava fought the urge to lean away from the clear menace in Connor's pose. "Let's get one thing perfectly straight," he said softly. His face was set in fierce lines, and his multi-colored eyes glowed with fiery intensity.

Ava hypnotically lifted her gaze to his face, overwhelmed by his sheer physical presence. Arousal tingled through her at his proximity and his obvious strength. "Just because I won't, doesn't mean I don't *want* to."

Connor shoved up and off her desk, then strode purposefully away. Ava was struck speechless by his words as she watched the play of his glutes beneath his snug cargo pants. Her heart still beat erratically in her chest and either she'd had a major sugar crash from her hard boiled egg breakfast or all the blood in her head had rushed south to a very under-used body part.

One question kept circling in her suddenly light-headed brain: Did he just say he wanted *her*?

# CHAPTER 2

*S*mooth, *real smooth, Con.*

Nothing like blurting out the fact that you had the hots for your co-worker. Not to mention opening the company up to a potential sexual harassment suit. Not to mention he'd managed to keep his insane attraction to her under wraps for nine months and in one unguarded moment, he'd undone months of keeping his shit together and being the man he wanted to be. Connor wanted to thunk his head against his desk.

Instead, he did what was familiar and retreated into code and computers. Code didn't lie. Code didn't throw out confusing signals. Code didn't make an ass of itself. Code was just there doing its job. Not bothering anyone. Code could be scrambled, sure. But once you unraveled the pattern, the truth behind the code was evident.

Con ran backup security scans on the Stone Consulting system while he dug into the other job that Jack had given him.

José Fernandez. Now Con remembered where he'd heard the name. Fernandez was currently waiting on Senate confirmation as Deputy Secretary of Labor. He was a champion of civil rights and had crusaded for migrant farm worker rights locally in Monterey County before launching his political career, moving on to the state of California, and now Washington DC.

On the surface, Fernandez seemed like a great choice and a shoo-in for the job. As Con did the initial check on the politician, the guy seemed to have a golden career. But if Stone Consulting was investigating him, Con had to believe there was something about Fernandez that had set off Jack's bullshit meter.

Congress was in recess through the Thanksgiving holiday. Jack wanted the report done as soon as possible which told Connor that some people in DC weren't on vacation yet.

Hours later, Con still couldn't get Ava out of his head. Her jaw had dropped when he'd confessed that he wanted her. Surprise had blanketed her gorgeous face. She had round cheeks, a long nose, black eyebrows always slightly arched as if she found the world around her amusing, eyes so dark—they were the color of the night sky on the foggy coast—and plump full lips painted a bright cherry red. Usually her mouth was curved in a half-smile but earlier her lips had formed a clear *oh* before she snapped her teeth shut.

He'd never seen Ava anything other than professional, but sometimes he sensed a melancholy in her. Today her eyes had glittered with temper when he'd clumsily tried to apologize for Jack's comment. Now Connor couldn't stop picturing her wantonly spread-eagled on Jack's desk, her elegant hands clutched around his biceps, her red nails digging into his arms, and her sweetly rounded ass perched on the edge of the desk as Con powered in and out of her. Shit.

All the blood in his body pooled in his groin. Awesome. He had a fucking hard on. At work. While he fantasized about his brother's assistant. Could this day get any more wacked?

Connor absently watched the code from their server scroll across his screen. He frowned as an odd bit of text caught his eye. He stopped the rapidly scrolling information and backed up to the unfamiliar code. He took a screenshot and then kept going.

But that niggling sense of something out of place had him separating his screen into two different views, he kept an eye on the scrolling code while on the other screen he stared at that little piece of wrongness.

The short, innocuous command did not belong in the middle of the other code on the screen. And he knew it wasn't his. So who or what was trying, and not succeeding, thanks to his little encryption lock, to break into their system?

Connor shifted back to the scrolling code to search for more attempts at illegal forays or bits of commands that didn't belong. He needed to review all the evidence and make sure he had all his facts and the proof to back it up before he took any suspicions to Jack.

He started a backtrace to find out where the attempted hack had originated. And he set up an alert for any more possible breaches from the same IP address. Then he programmed a little surprise for the next time they tried to hack the company.

He thought about taking this information to Jack right away, but he wanted to have more concrete evidence and a plan in place to fix it before he exposed his findings to his brother. *Deeds not words.*

While he continued to monitor the code, he found three

more instances where someone had tried to break into Stone Consulting. Connor made a quick printout of the illicit hack attempts on their system. This was beyond bad.

❧

AVA FINISHED TYPING the report regarding GHR's aid on the earthquake-ravaged island of Port-du-Bois. Jess Stone had just returned a few weeks ago from the disaster area along with their new employee Colin Davies.

Jess and Colin appeared to have hit it off on the op. The rumor was they'd gotten busy on Jack's desk. Ava blushed as heat spread through her body just thinking about Jack's comment. Even with no one to see her.

She needed to think about other things. More important things than her unwelcome and unrequited attraction to Connor Stone. Let's face it, her infatuation was going nowhere. Until today, she had no idea that he even noticed she was a woman. But she loved this job and if she got involved with Connor even briefly, and if it ended badly when they were done, she'd be the one out the door. Jack wasn't about to fire his brother.

She needed to shut down that line of thought right now.

Instead, Ava focused on her work—rewarding work that fulfilled her. Jack had given her the freedom to research philanthropies and initiate a new beneficiary for GHR. She had found the perfect recipient for a cause she whole-heartedly believed in. *S.S.A.F.E*, Security, Shelter, and Freedom for the Exploited, was an organization that helped trafficked women and children reintegrate into society after they were freed from slavery.

She had written the proposal to show how GHR could support the organization and before the year was out the philanthropy would become the newest beneficiary of GHR's generosity. *Ava* had done that.

Jack knew her background. He knew about Maria and the others. Her reason for wanting to work for GHR and her need to atone.

He had also promised that one day soon, once she had more training, she would be able to go on relief missions. So Ava had started CrossFit training, soaked up knowledge of all aspects of Global Humanitarian Relief's practices, and mentally catalogued everything that went on at the main company, GHR, and it's less altruistic subsidiary, Stone Consulting.

Actually, she had little idea what Stone Consulting did. Jack handled everything except the finance numbers. She knew Stone Consulting made a lot of money. And some of their clients were likely governments, based on the acronyms on their Profit and Loss statements. Beyond that, the shadowy company was opaque. The workings and job specifics of Stone Consulting were completely obscured from her.

The office was quiet. Riley was out of the country on an op and everyone else had left on vacation for the holidays. Since her parents had gone back to Sinaloa for a month leaving her alone for the next few weeks, Ava had volunteered to man the office. Thanksgiving was only six days away and the entire office was closed next week so that Jack's employees could go home to their families.

Jack Stone valued family. Ava knew that from his dogged pursuit to get all his siblings working for GHR. He'd finally succeeded, and the last holdout, Jess, had left the FBI and come to work for him a few months ago.

Jack had departed right before lunch, muttering to himself about arrogance, payback favors, and something else she couldn't quite hear. Ava was pretty sure that she and Connor, who was secreted back in his office with his computers after making an ass of himself, were the only ones left in the fourth floor office suite.

She read through the report one last time. Jack usually reviewed the GHR reports, confirming mission details and conclusions, sometimes changing a word or two, before she hit send. But today he'd been in a hurry and asked Ava to double check this one.

Ava always took note of the altered meaning when he made changes. Then when he was completely satisfied with the contents, she sent the highly-encrypted file to someone, somewhere in DC. The email was generic with no identifier as to agency or corporation. To her eye, there wasn't any information that could be considered classified. But based on the level of encryption, she figured there must be information that wasn't readily available to the general public.

She wasn't stupid. She'd figured out after two months on the job that Stone Consulting's income supported Global Humanitarian Relief's efforts. Stone Consulting was the moneymaker with no written files or traceable evidence of the work performed. But the company's profits allowed GHR to do a lot of good, as proven by Jess and Colin's report from Port-du-Bois. They had handed out tens of thousands of packets of both water purification tablets and seeds to the disaster-ravaged population. The people of Port-du-Bois were already better off for the good that GHR had done while they were on the island.

It hadn't escaped Ava's notice that the head of the country had also conveniently died of natural causes while they were there.

Ava didn't know if that was related or not, and she'd

decided after reading about Henri LeRoy's atrocities in this report, somehow none of his various misdeeds were in the international news, that she didn't care to delve too deeply into what had happened. But sometimes she did wonder if it were smart to ignore the mystery of Stone Consulting.

Ava double checked every detail one last time and then with a deep breath, she hit send.

She had one final task to finish before she could go work out. Jack had given her a Stone Consulting report that needed to be sent...somewhere. He'd given her the handwritten note with a request that she shred the paper as soon as the document was in the computer, send the report, and then delete the sent email.

Ava typed the report quickly. Jack had hesitated before handing her the handwritten note but she couldn't figure out why. The entire report and email consisted of one short paragraph: *SC is investigating Subject F more deeply through online records. Going after living proof of wrongdoing. Beyond witness, no other physical evidence exists at this time. Will have updated report or hopefully evidence in custody before Thanksgiving.*

Ava typed the email, hit send, and promptly deleted all references on her computer. Jack hadn't signed the email. It was sent from a one time account that was deleted as soon as she transmitted the 'report.' Ava took the innocuous piece of paper and put it through the high security, random particle shredder, until it was 46,000 bits of confetti.

This was a big step for Ava. He had never entrusted her with the other, more secret, aspects of the company and Ava felt a silly sense of pride. She'd moved to a new stage in learning the business. She was one step closer to her goal of helping people, saving people.

Ava hit the women's restroom and changed into her running clothes. It was time for her Workout of the Day.

GHR's office was located in the downtown area of Monterey. On the fourth floor, both Ava's reception area and Jack's office had a gorgeous view of the Monterey Bay and the very touristy marina. But what Ava loved most about the GHR office was the quick access to the beach and the ocean.

Ava ran along the cold wet sand of Municipal Beach. She let the sand kick up and splatter her legs. The brisk sea breeze, scented with salt and seaweed, buffeted her body and swept through her hair. Sweat sheened her face and the mist from the ocean caused her usually restrained hair to curl wildly. Her hair was a tumbled mass around her face, totally unprofessional.

The running shorts allowed her the freedom to really fly. Her breasts were restrained in a heavy-duty Nike sports bra that would take an act of God to get her out of, but at least she wouldn't be flopping all over the place while she ran full out. Since Jack wanted her to stay late tonight, he'd told her to take time in the afternoon to get her beach workout in.

It was tempting to hop on the Monterey Bay Coastal Trail and run down to Seaside and back but she had to be back in the office to wait for Riley's once-a-day check-in.

She'd already done her workout: sprints, lunges, pull-ups on the bar at the playground, and burpees. As a result her heart pounded and her thighs trembled. She focused on the effects of her workout on her body. Anything to stop remembering his words and get the look in Connor's eyes out of her mind. The physical exercise was the perfect antidote to her wayward thoughts and the uncomfortable, edgy, itchy sensations nagging her.

*Doesn't mean I don't want. Doesn't mean I don't want.*

Ava tried not to read sexual craving into his confession,

but it was hard when she remembered the heat in his intense stare.

A prickle of awareness crept along her neck. The usually crowded beach, even on a November afternoon, was basically deserted. With the exception of a few crazy couples frolicking in the frigid waves or passed out on their beach towels, the tourist crowds were gone for the day, getting ready for dinner or giving their kids baths. The dive boats had all come in for the night and the water was too placid for surfers.

Seagulls squawked. The waves shushed gently on the shore. The traffic on Del Monte Avenue just beyond the sand was muted. Though everything seemed deserted, Ava couldn't help but feel like she wasn't alone.

She stopped, put her hands on her knees and bent slightly at the waist. The position gave her the chance to casually look between her legs and behind her. But she didn't see anyone suspicious and no one who hadn't been there as she'd jogged by.

Ava plopped down into the sand and decided to do her post-workout stretches right here while the waves lapped at the shore. She stretched her legs out in front of her and bent at the waist to rest her forehead on her knees. Through slitted eyes she surveyed the beach again. And still no one looked out of place.

So why the hell did it feel like someone was watching her?

Ava twisted and stretched as she warmed down, trying desperately to shake off the feeling of being hunted. The sensation triggered more awareness. She didn't feel like the watcher was ogling her short shorts or body. The unknown gaze felt desperate and just a little bit malevolent.

*Dios*, she'd let her imagination get the best of her. Ava

tried to shrug it off as she brushed the sand from her legs. Then she untied the office key from her shoelace and clutched it in her hand, the jagged edge sticking through her index and middle finger. She began a light jog back to the office. To her mind, the sooner she arrived the better.

Within ten minutes, she was at the front door of their building. She peered at the reflection of the street behind her in the glass, searching for a tail, searching for anyone who didn't belong, but nothing suspicious jumped out at her.

Ava shoved the key in the lock and quickly let herself into the building. She leaned back against the door, closed her eyes, and breathed a quick sigh of relief at the odd sense of safety she felt once she was behind the locked door.

"Where've you been?"

Ava shrieked and jumped back into a fighting stance before she registered it was only Connor.

Her heart was pounding hard and blood rushed in her ears as her body dumped a boatload of adrenaline into her system.

"Holy crap, you scared me." Ava willed the rapid rat-a-tat-tat of her heart into a slower, steadier rhythm.

"What was that all about?" Connor had eased back so he was a few feet away. And after a quick glance at her body in the skintight running top and shorts, he averted his gaze to the old-fashioned marquee that listed the buildings occupants. "Never mind. I need to talk to Jack."

Ava tried to stem the disappointment that followed. As if he sensed her turmoil, Connor put more distance between them. She might be shy, but she was also a toucher. And Connor always seemed to be moving away from her, not closer. Which conversely made her want to reach out and grab him.

Great. Now she was imagining physically accosting Connor Stone. And why, oh why, couldn't she get images of touching Connor out of her brain?

What had he asked? Jack, he wanted to talk to Jack. "He's gone."

"Shit." Connor stood perfectly still. One blunt tipped hand cupped his neck while he frowned at the large marble squares of the entry floor. She had the image that inside his stiff body, he was mentally pacing like a large lion.

His entire form was preternaturally still, but his muscles, of which there were many, rippled beneath his cargo pants. His biceps strained against the hem of his short sleeve t-shirt, veins popped in sharp relief against the definition of his forearms, even his neck had sensually distinct muscles. But even with all those muscles on display, the most attractive muscle Connor Stone displayed was still his brain.

His mind moved at warp speed and the way he processed information was somehow sexy as hell. So okay, his body rocked too. But there was something about all that brute strength wrapped around a brain with rapidly-firing synapses that fueled her attraction to him.

Her body heated, her pulse sped up and thudded in the base of her throat as she waited for him to sort out whatever he needed.

"This can't wait," Connor muttered. "I have to know now."

"What can't wait?" Ava asked with bewilderment.

Connor charged toward the utilitarian stairwell, eschewing the old-fashioned elevator with the slow moving cars and heavy ornate brass doors. Ava followed behind him, trying and failing not to admire the full extent of his muscles.

Jack had given Ava clear instructions: Connor was in

charge. He'd also said he didn't think anything major would come up while he was unreachable. So she followed.

Their footsteps clanged in the eerily silent stairwell as Connor sprinted up the steps. Ava clambered up the stairs behind him.

"I need to know what everyone is working on." Connor barreled through the access door to the fourth floor then held the door open until Ava could finish climbing. She slid through the doorway and hustled to her office desk.

Ava couldn't figure out why he was so upset. They really didn't have much going on right this moment. Just Riley delivering school supplies and whatever Jack was working on.

Connor was pacing back and forth. The action so unusual for Connor that she just stared. Why was he so upset?

Finally he leaned over her desk. "We have a breach."

Ava dropped into the chair behind her heavy wooden desk, the computer screen to her right had gone to sleep, and all the physical files were locked away in the vault in Jack's office. "That's not possible," she blurted without thinking. Connor was great with computers.

He blinked as if he hadn't really been seeing her, and his laser focus narrowed in on Ava. "You wouldn't think so. But I'm positive we had someone try to worm through our firewalls."

Ava leaned back at the vehemence of Connor's words. She glanced around the silent and empty office. They were the only ones still at work, but she still didn't feel comfortable discussing his problem out in the open. "We should go in Jack's office. The walls are sound-proofed."

Ava pulled the large key ring from the bottom of her purse. When she was dressed in her four-inch heels, sling-

back black patent pumps with a sexy peep toe, Connor towered over her five-foot-five frame. Right now, wearing only her running shoes, he was enormous and his frustration was overpowering.

"Excellent idea." Connor stood next to her as she inserted the metal key into the old-fashioned lock. She tried not to notice the immense heat he generated as she clumsily fumbled the keys.

Connor crowded behind her, and the heat from his body surrounded hers. He awkwardly curled his palm around her bicep and held her still.

Ava froze. He'd never touched her before. Ever. He wasn't a toucher. Connor tended to keep his distance, and the unfamiliar clasp of his fingers against her bare arm, set off a riot of conflicting emotions. Thrill, surprise, longing, heat.

Ava shook off the inappropriate feelings. She needed to gain a little distance, and a whole lot of perspective. His earlier admission and the incident on the beach must have rattled her more than she thought.

Without volition, she released a little hum of reaction to the sensations from the touch of his hand and curbed the impulse to touch him back.

 on almost swallowed his tongue. He had never been this close to Ava when she was dressed so casually. While at work she wore demure suits and pumps, a little on the formal side for casual Monterey but she rocked the traditional office look. Right now in short running shorts that showcased her lean brown legs and her fantastic rounded rear end, and a tight spandex top that hugged her breasts lovingly, her amazing body was revealed.

She hid a serious bombshell figure with lithe feminine curves beneath those boxy suits. With her hair down and curling around her face, and her cheeks flushed from her workout, all he could think about was how he'd like to press her up against Jack's door and make her face flush for another reason.

Her skin was warm and soft beneath his hand. He didn't touch people. And yet, he was having the most difficult time forcing himself to release her arm. He wanted to smooth his palm down her silky skin and thread their fingers together and hold on tight.

As her body reacted to his innocuous touch, he was

tempted to sweep back the errant curl that clung to her neck, and tuck her hair behind the shell of her ear, then whisper sexy nothings to her and see if he could make her crave Jack's forbidden warning as much as he did. Their bodies swayed perilously close together as the air around them seemed to thicken with sexual awareness.

Shit. He needed to shut those thoughts down. The company had a serious problem and he was too busy pawing Ava to figure it out. He needed to pay attention. Now. This was his chance to prove to Jack that he was worthy. Worthy of the Stone name, worthy of the responsibility of being in charge. That worthiness did not include fucking Ava on Jack's desk.

Ava fumbled the key to Jack's office again and Connor finally clued into the fact that she had seemed very unsettled since she'd entered the building's front door. "Are you okay?"

"Yes." But her gaze darted furtively around as if she were searching for a threat. She finally got the key in the lock, opened the door to Jack's office, and scurried inside.

The behavior was so out of character that against his better judgment, he shifted closer to her, tensed, and searched the lengthening shadows of her outer office for any sign of danger, ready to protect her. But nothing looked out of place or alarming. Finally, he pushed into Jack's office and closed the door with a resolute thump. "What's wrong?"

"It's...nothing."

But it wasn't. "Tell me anyway."

She stammered, "I—I felt like someone was watching me while I did my workout."

Connor's thoughts quickened. He'd already identified attempted cyber intrusions, could there also be an imminent physical attack?

Once again, Con needed more information. Ava didn't strike him as reactionary or particularly paranoid. He'd barely identified the cyber threat before she'd gone for her workout. Could they possibly be related? He was pretty sure that he knew the answers to the questions he was about to ask, but he wanted to make sure. "Do you do the same workout regularly?"

"No."

"Same time or same path?"

"Not really. I do CrossFit so I vary my workout and today I just happened to be on the beach early since Jack wanted me to stay in the office late."

"So you thought you were being watched. Do you think you were followed?" Con persisted.

"I'm sure it was nothing."

"Do you frequently suffer from feelings of paranoia or delusions?" Con already knew the answer but he wanted to goad her.

"What? Of course not." Ava clenched her fists as if she was trying to restrain from hitting him and the slightly panicked look was replaced by the fiery passion he'd invoked earlier today.

"Then trust your instincts." Paired with the fact that he was positive that someone was trying to breach their cyber security, the hackles on Con's neck raised. Something was very, very wrong here. And Ava needed to be on her guard.

His words deflated her animosity. She straightened her shoulders and nodded. "Okay."

They stood close together, huddled next to the door, and spoke in hushed tones as if unwilling to let anyone else hear what they were discussing. But as soon as she acquiesced, Con realized the intimacy of their position.

He stepped away from Ava and focused on his other

problem. He needed to talk to Jack. "Did Jack leave any contact information?"

Ava shook her head, the messy black curls brushed the bare curve of her neck and Con found himself getting distracted all over again. "Just his cell."

Con had tried Jack's cell with no luck. It was only about six p.m. Jack should have picked up. "Where is he?"

"I have no idea." Ava tilted her head and pursed her lips. "We could check with Shane and find out what flight plan he filed."

"Good idea." Con pulled out his cell and called Shane's cell. But Shane didn't answer either.

Con frowned. None of this made sense. Jack wasn't usually completely unreachable. Unless he was still in the air. "I don't like it. He didn't leave any other contact information?"

"No. He said you were in charge."

"Dammit." Con paced around Jack's office, trying to work out what to do next. But when Ava put a hand on the doorknob as if she planned to leave, he stopped her cold with the flat of his palm.

Ava snapped, "What do you want from me?"

Inappropriate images popped into his mind. "Nothing I can have," he muttered.

Ava blinked, then pretended she didn't hear him. She stayed silent. Which worked just fine for Connor. He couldn't have her, so he needed to just get over it.

Con glanced out the picture window into the encroaching darkness. It was late. And then he wondered why Ava was still here.

"Why aren't you out of the office already?" Con's eyes narrowed.

"Jack needed me to stay."

"So late?"

"Jack wanted me to wait for a check-in call from Riley. Normally he would take it. He's supposed to call—" She glanced at the Garmin Forerunner watch on her wrist. "—in the next half an hour to an hour."

Con prowled toward her as he strategized out loud. "Okay. While you're waiting you can help me go through the list of recent Stone Consulting jobs."

"Actually, I can't."

"What do you mean? I'm in charge. I need that information."

"I said I can't, not I won't." Ava crossed her arms defensively over her chest. Connor tried to ignore the way the action plumped her breasts out the neckline of the tight top. *Shit, focus on the problems, Con.*

"Why?"

"I don't have clearance."

Connor frowned. "But…you're Jack's assistant."

"I don't have access to certain files." She raised an elegant black eyebrow as if making a more subtle inference. Could she really mean that she didn't see all the information that went through GHR and Stone Consulting?

"Spell it out for me," Connor said deliberately in a low, commanding voice.

Ava pushed away from the wall where Con practically had her cornered and put some distance between them. He was distracted again by her sleek, smooth legs and the tight spandex top that snugged her waist and cupped her breasts lovingly. She was curvy in all the right places. Her unique scent, floral perfume and slightly sweaty woman, wafted in the air and wrapped around his senses, distracting him even more. Was the office shrinking?

"Stone Consulting jobs are beyond my security clearance."

She still hadn't said shit. "Ava," Connor growled.

Ava edged away from Con and roamed around the office. "Fine. Jack handles all the Stone Consulting reports himself. He types them, emails them from secure accounts that I don't have access to and then shreds them. And if he keeps a record of them, I have no idea where. He must have them somewhere, but I have never seen them."

"Paranoid bastard." Con knew that Jack was a secretive son of a bitch but that was extreme even for Jack. Was there a more sinister explanation? How could Con figure out what was going on without knowledge of Stone Consulting jobs?

*Problem solve, Con.* All Con could do was reconstruct what he did know.

"The only reason I know that the jobs exist is because I edit the spreadsheet for the company accountant and know that Stone Consulting actually supports the efforts of GHR," she said sharply. "But most of the time I don't see any job details and I am not privy to the clients or the results."

Connor blew out an exasperated breath.

Then she hesitated.

"What?"

"Jack did have me send a classified report today but it really wasn't a report. It was only a few sentences." Ava had roamed over by Jack's desk. She ran a fingertip over the edge of the desk then straightened the blotter and replaced an errant pen in the cup holder at the edge of the blotter. "I can't imagine a report I sent today could have anything to do with your breach."

She was likely right.

However, the odds that the problems were related to

GHR business were slim. The reason someone was trying to get into their system through the backdoor was far more likely something to do with Stone Consulting. Which she apparently had no knowledge of except for this one report. Jack frequently piggy-backed intelligence reports about political climate and military movements where they donated goods and services onto the more philanthropic GHR jobs. Maybe Con could piece together what was going on with her knowledge of GHR's missions and glean some idea of what other information Jack had accumulated for Stone Consulting.

Another thought occurred to Con. Jack had asked him to look into José Fernandez this morning. It seemed unlikely that their problems stemmed from the investigation of Fernandez since Jack just asked Con, but he couldn't rule it out.

First, he'd start with the one piece of Stone Consulting business that she knew about. "Can you show me the email?"

"Actually he had me delete everything."

"Everything?"

She was silent for a few more seconds as if debating how much to tell him.

"Really?" Connor prodded. "Is that standard operating procedure?"

Ava flushed. "I've never worked on any Stone Consulting reports." She twisted a lock of hair around her long elegant finger. "So I don't know but I would guess that it is SOP."

"Well I really need you to tell me what was in the report," Connor prompted.

She still hesitated.

He understood that it was a big step for her but— "Jack left me in charge."

"It was...vague." Ava looked uncomfortable for a few seconds. "I figured that's why Jack let me send it. I really couldn't figure anything from the contents."

"Can you try to remember word for word?"

Ava closed her eyes, her black lashes fanned across her olive-skinned cheeks, as she attempted to recall the few sentences. "Something about a subject, retrieving evidence, and more information by Thanksgiving."

"I need the exact words," Connor said impatiently. A small detail could make the difference between garbage and concrete, actionable intelligence. She finally recited the email verbatim. Very slowly.

*"SC is investigating Subject F more deeply through online records. Going after living proof of wrongdoing. Beyond witness, no other physical evidence exists at this time. Will have updated report or hopefully evidence in custody before Thanksgiving."*

Con mentally reviewed the text. Subject F. Fernandez would be his guess. Could the esteemed activist that Con was investigating be behind the current intrusion and Ava's feeling of being watched?

"Does that help?" Ava stare was direct and uncompromising.

He wasn't supposed to tell anyone about his investigation. He couldn't confirm that the email did make sense and it was likely connected to his orders. And it was possible that it was connected to her sense of being watched. However right now it was all speculation. He had nothing specific he could share.

"Connor?" She stared him down until they both broke eye contact. Unfortunately, they both focused on the same object at the same time. As one their gaze shifted to Jack's desk. Connor thought about that flush. Thought about the images that kept taunting him. Of her, of him, locked together in a passionate embrace. For a long taut moment, he wondered if she were imagining the same things.

He thought about the sleek, smooth glide of his palm over her skin. And wondered if she was as sleek and smooth in other more intimate places.

Shit. This was going to be a long night. Because he couldn't let her go yet. "I need you to go over some more information with me before you leave."

"What do you need to know?"

"I want the mission and location of everyone in the office right now. And maybe the last mission they were involved in."

Ava sighed.

"Do you have any place you need to be?" Connor asked with regret. *Like a date?* He hoped the answer was no.

It was, after all, a Friday night.

Ava sighed. "No," she replied softly. "I'm all yours."

He wished.

# CHAPTER 4

Two hours later, they'd gone through all the missions that Global Humanitarian Relief had completed over the last six months. From those missions, he could make some educated guesses about what kinds of reports Stone Consulting had submitted.

The few that really jumped out at him were Jess's little foray to Port-du-Bois, Riley's current mission in the Philippines, and Jack's current status as MIA. Not to mention his own investigation of Fernandez.

Ava had identified a new philanthropy beneficiary, S.S.A.F.E., but so far they hadn't done any work for them yet. So there couldn't be any connection there.

But Con thought about that new philanthropy and the obvious connection to José Fernandez. Connor knew Ava had firsthand knowledge of the incident, the abduction of the children of immigrants, that catapulted Fernandez into the career that had gotten him where he was today.

He needed to ask her some questions. But he hated to bring up something that he figured, based on her choice of philanthropy, still haunted her.

"So I couldn't help but wonder what made you choose S.S.A.F.E.?" Con was pretty sure that he knew but he wasn't about to tell her that he'd read her file.

Ava didn't say anything, just averted her gaze and licked her lips. He'd spent enough time watching her and thinking about her, that he didn't think she was the type to prevaricate. On the other hand, this was the most time he'd ever spent ever talking to Ava. She was sharp, smart, had an excruciating eye for detail and he wanted to jump her bad.

Then she spoke and all thoughts of jumping her disappeared. "When I was fifteen, my friend was taken."

Con's first thought was 'thank god it wasn't you.' His second instinct was to question. "How did they know she didn't just run away?"

But Ava was already shaking her head. "No."

"Okay." He wanted to wrap her in his arms protect her from whatever she was going to tell him next. The temptation to stop her from remembering was strong. But he needed her firsthand account. So he rubbed a hand over his rumbling stomach and eased back into Jack's chair, giving her the illusion of space. "So tell me."

"My parents were migrant workers."

Which of course he knew. But she must have worked hard to eradicate her accent because there was no inflection or cadence to her words that would indicate English wasn't her first language.

He waited as she gathered her thoughts. "When I was fifteen, there were several girls snatched from our community on their way to the fields after school. On the day my best friend, Maria, and the other girls were taken, I was home sick."

*Several* girls. His heart nearly stopped as he realized she

could have been one of them. Had she been spared solely because she'd been sick?

Connor's heart thumped hard in his chest. His mind continued to scroll through possibilities and probabilities. Although he already knew the basics of the story from his research on Fernandez, he prompted her. She was a source of information he couldn't access online. Her recollection might not be perfect but impressions and intuition could be far more valuable than dry facts on a website or in a newspaper article. Maybe he could learn something from her memories about what happened eight years ago.

"What did the police say about the abductions?"

She snorted. "No one cared about illegal immigrant girls. The families couldn't afford to make a big noise in the media. The first thing cops do is look at family and friends. Her parents were likely to get deported back to Mexico where they would have no hope of ever finding her."

But José Fernandez had made the girls' disappearances his call to arms.

Again Connor wanted her insider view of the case. "So what happened?"

"We never saw any of the girls again." Ava's mouth turned down. "The more superstitious whispered about *El Chupacabra* but I knew...those girls weren't taken by any mythical creature. They were taken by evil."

"I wasn't here then so I don't remember."

Just because he'd made the leap to Fernandez as subject F, didn't mean he wanted her to make that connection. Besides, Jack had made it clear that he was not to talk to anyone about his investigation into José Fernandez. Which meant he couldn't share his suspicions that subject F was likely Fernandez.

"It became big news a few months later because José

Fernandez, the local Union organizer for migrant workers, made it his mission to draw attention to the lack of services available and justice for immigrants."

Con nodded. "He's supposed to be confirmed as Deputy Secretary of Labor after the recess."

"Yes." She grimaced, her gaze skittered to the picture window and then back to him. "He's waiting on approval from the Senate."

There was a hint of something in her voice. Disdain, ambivalence, loathing but he wasn't quite sure.

"You don't like him?" Jack thought Fernandez needed a deep look and his brother was known for intuitive thinking.

"I think he used a deplorable situation to advance his own political agenda. And something about him always set off my squick meter." She rubbed her index finger along the outside length of her forearm clearly lost in her memories.

Connor was silent for a moment as he examined implications and patterns, shifting the events of eight years ago and the current situation through filters and reaching for a connection. But he kept getting distracted by thoughts of Ava as a young, almost victim.

"That's why you wanted to work for GHR." He understood the desire to change or make up for what happened in the past. Hell wasn't that what the last nine months had been about?

She kept her gaze averted. "The opportunity to be able to make a difference both here and around the world is a powerful draw."

But Con was astute enough to recognize that while she might say she wanted to make a difference, her true goal was atonement. Wasn't he still trying to atone for his awful teenaged mistakes? He could see inside her to that kernel of guilt that lived where no one, perhaps not even Ava, knew it existed.

Ava rubbed her hand over the center of her breastbone. Connor tried to ignore the little ping of arousal. He was a total dog for getting turned on while she was obviously still upset.

"I'm sorry about your friend." He suppressed the urge to take her in his arms and comfort her, and said gently, "But I'm very glad it wasn't you."

She was perched on Jack's desk and Con's hand was mere inches from her knee. The need to touch her, to confirm she was here now and she was okay, burned like a physical ache. Con put his hand on her knee and squeezed to relay his thanks that she was okay.

But the move startled her. "Oh!" She jerked her knee back at his touch, her eyes wide and round.

Truly, his only thought had been comfort, but the second he touched her skin, electricity arced between them, hot and sizzling.

"Shit." Connor went to push back Jack's chair, but Ava's foot got tangled up in the chair, and she lost her balance. Con's hands came up in a classic 'hands off' gesture. But it was too late. Ava fell forward. While trying to stop her from face planting in his lap, he managed to press his palms right on her perfect-sized breasts. Which startled her even worse and horrified him. He yanked his hands away. "Jesus. Sorry!"

She tried to pull back, but that action backfired. Somehow, she landed in his lap her knee digging into his hip, but without hitting his erection, thank God.

But her forward momentum pressed her very generous D-cups right into his face and his nose ended up buried in her cleavage. The scent of woman hit him like a sucker punch. Her spicy sweet floral perfume, the salty tang from a good workout, and the tantalizing fragrance that was all Ava, swirled around him, intoxicating him until all he could think about, all he could do was take what he'd been stalwartly ignoring for the last nine months.

Connor curled his fingers around her hips and pressed a very chaste kiss against the mound of her breast. He moaned into her supple skin and couldn't help himself, he swirled his tongue over the top of her sweet, salty flesh.

Her breath caught and lifted her breasts like an offering to the gods, and he was powerless to do anything other than worship her. With wet, open-mouthed kisses he forged a path along the scoop neckline of her sports top, each suction of his lips and swipe of his tongue elicited another hushed, fervent gasp.

Her fingers clutched his head even as her hot sex sank down over the erection straining the fly of his pants. There was no protest in her actions, only a silent request for more. So Con indulgently suckled the delicate skin along her collarbone. The sweet musk of feminine arousal drifted from her body. His cock was harder than a silicone motherboard.

All his cognitive thought had arrowed to his groin. As if a virus swept through his system, common sense was wiped out and replaced with everything Ava. Her nearness, her feminine scent, her sheer sensuality. The images that he'd tried to suppress earlier came roaring back, flooding his mind and turning him one giant throbbing hormone. His body was intent on one thing. Making those images a reality.

Yesterday, he wouldn't have even considered touching her. But one random comment from Jack about sex on his desk, with Ava, and with everything else that had happened today…sex with Ava was all Con could think about. As if her touch unlocked a door in his mind, an avalanche of memories tumbled through his brain. Ava appreciating his mind as well as his body. The sweet bow of her mouth as she quietly smiled at his jokes. The curve of her lashes against her cheek as she hid her gaze from his. The little crease between her brows when she concentrated fiercely.

And that involuntary hitch in her breath this morning when he told her he wanted her.

Ava writhed over his cock, her running shorts a thin, silky barrier to her wet, waiting heat. He knew she was on board with his actions and his kisses when her clever, elegant fingers eased under the hem of his plain t-shirt. He had to stop kissing her skin to allow her to rip the t-shirt off and pull the cotton over his head. While he couldn't touch her with his mouth, he cupped her breasts and thumbed her diamond hard nipples through the slippery spandex top.

She scraped her fingernails over his back and smoothed her palm over the tense muscles of his pectorals, his body jumping at the sensual touch. And while his body rejoiced, his brain kept working.

This was a bad idea. But damn, she felt good.

*WHAT THE HELL was she doing?* Ava knew this was a bad idea. And yet, so not a bad idea. She had been crushing on Connor Stone since she met him. Tonight, talking about Maria brought it all home. All the feelings she'd had when her friend had been kidnapped. And when Maria hadn't been found, Ava had resolved to live life fully.

Ava's thoughts ran rampant. Pictures bulleted through her mind and she thought of all the times she'd turned away from her attraction to Connor. All the times she'd ducked her head and averted her gaze, unwilling to show him that she wanted him. But here she was, sitting on Connor Stone's lap, and if the erection bulging against her swollen and ready sex was any indication he was as aroused and interested as she was. He wanted *her*. And all her determination to seize the day coalesced into one giant resolution.

Ava knelt over Connor and finally made a move. *She* made the move and pressed her mouth to his.

*Seize the moment.*

Connor's mouth was warm, supple, and responsive.

He kissed the way he approached everything. With attention to detail and deliberate movements. His large hand cupped her cheek, and his fingers rested against the skin behind her ear, each pad a buzz of energy as if he were wired. His thumb brushed down the length of her nose and the swirl of brown and gold starbursts dazzled her as he hypnotically held her gaze. She was trapped by his overwhelming energy. Her entire body simmered with arousal, all pent-up sexual want and nearly a year of suppressed sexual feelings.

His lips were softer than she expected, and they curved into a smug smile.

"What?" she asked.

"I like it."

The first brush of his mouth had been sweet, tender. Now, as if he couldn't wait any longer, Connor surged up, slanted his head and devoured her mouth. His tongue licked at her lips, and aggressively demanded entrance. He tasted of coffee with a single creamer.

Connor curled his hands beneath her ass and lifted her up with ease. A visceral thrill rocketed through her at the unconscious display of strength. He deposited her on the

desktop without breaking off the deep, drugging kisses and stepped between her spread thighs as if he belonged there. Then he slid his hot, hard palms up the sides of her spandex workout top and lightly cupped her breasts, right through the tightly constraining material.

All the blood in her body rushed to her sex with dizzying speed. Ava's head went light as she swayed against him.

She paused, tried to think about what was happening here, what was the right action to take. But all that seemed to occupy her mind was the hard feel of his thighs between hers, the firm pressure of his hands on her breasts, and the wet suction of his mouth.

Talking about her friend Maria had brought home the fact that life was short. Hadn't she taken that to heart when Maria disappeared? Ava had started taking her classes more seriously, determined to make something of herself, determined to make her life count. To live the gift that she'd been granted to the fullest, a gift that her friend had been denied.

But lately, she'd been too complacent. Fallen into a routine, looking to the future so much that she forgot to live in the present.

The present was here in front of her, and she'd be a fool not to take advantage of what Connor Stone represented.

It had been months since she'd been out on a date and even longer since she'd had sex. She hadn't yet experienced her wild and crazy years. She'd lived at home while she went to college and just recently moved into her first apartment by herself. Her parents would still prefer that she live at home. The long-lasting legacy from Maria and the other girls spurred an irrational fear that Ava could be taken too.

So her sexual experience was limited to some fumbling dates in college. Since she started working for GHR she hadn't had time to find a boyfriend. She wasn't a partier or particularly social. She'd rather be at home cooking a good meal or reading a book or doing her CrossFit workouts than at a bar.

"What are we doing?" she murmured, needing to be sure that they were on the same wavelength.

"Indulging." He nuzzled the sensitive spot beneath her ear even as his hands skimmed around to her butt and pulled her tight against his even harder erection.

He felt so good. Warm and strong and *there*.

There to comfort her, there to hold her, there to take all her cares and worries and stress away. Connor Stone was the consistent one, the solid one, the steady guy who was around whenever anyone needed him. He quietly went about his business and supported everyone else in the company without complaint, without ever making a fuss. She wondered what kind of lover would he be? Then she wondered, who took care of him? Who supported him?

And she wanted, at least for this brief moment in time, to be the one he turned to. The one who took care of him. The one who looked out for him.

Ava's pulse thudded in her ears as if she'd done three WODs until she was wrung out. She had two choices, and only a few seconds to decide.

Her body was melting from the inside, every sweet kiss, every tender brush of his fingertips sent a cascade of sparklers through her and sent an answering pulse to her sex. It was hot and sweet and insane.

"Indulging is good," she finally replied. Her voice sounded as if she'd run a four-minute mile, raspy and husky. She'd be a total fool if she didn't seize the opportunity to have sex with him. She wasn't naive. There was no love involved here. At least not on Connor's part. But she had enough unrequited longing for both of them.

As if her consent unleashed restraint she didn't even know he was exerting, Connor dragged her spandex top up her body, the stubborn material clung to her skin, her breasts. "Arms up," he commanded guttural voice. His impatience was evident in his jerky movements as he struggled to remove her running top.

"You certainly didn't dress for seduction, did you?" he growled.

# CHAPTER 5

Thank God, Ava was on board. Con finally got the spandex to release its chastity grip on her smooth, sleek skin and he ripped the top over her head and tossed it behind him.

His breath caught at the bounty spread before him. Her breasts were heavy and full and round with gorgeous silver-dollar-sized areola the color of the pomegranate seeds he ate like candy, and the same deep shade as her mouth. Her lips were swollen and plump from the force of their kisses.

Her hands clutched at his shoulders and her nipples were just begging for his intimate kiss.

"Damn, you are beautiful." He delicately lapped at the aroused bud, then rolled the engorged button on his tongue. He plucked her other nipple in his long fingers and drew a breathy moan from her.

Triumph surged through him at her response. His cock ached and the heat from her sex nearly burned him with the intensity of her arousal.

Ava burrowed her hand between their bodies and began to unbutton his pants, even as he played with her breasts.

The scent of hot, aroused woman and underlay of the sea and sand, wrapped around his senses. He was full to bursting, his balls tingled and his cock throbbed with the need to bury himself deep in her slick channel.

Ava had managed to get his zipper down and reach into his briefs. Her long, cool fingers wrapped around his dick and all the blood in his head surged south. Fucking A, he was harder than the barrel of his Glock. Locked and loaded and ready to blow.

"Stand up," he gutted out.

She pushed off the desktop but didn't let go, her hand working him, stroking slowly, clearly trying to drive him over the edge. Her breasts hung in his face, and it took a Herculean act to ignore the temptation to bury his face in her cleavage.

Connor clasped his hands around her hips and shoved her tiny running shorts to her ankles. His pants and underwear were caught at his thighs, and her hands were busy cupping his balls and massaging him.

"Jesus."

Ava had managed to get one foot free of her shorts. Connor scooped his hands underneath her thighs and shifted her so she lay back on the desk, her legs spread out on top of the cordovan leather blotter. He made the mistake of glancing down and the sight of her ruby red pussy, dark curls glistening with her juice, and her tawnier fingers wrapped around his white erection nearly caused him to blow right then. A drop of pre-come leaked onto her fist. He wanted to pound inside her with an ache that was unprecedented.

"You're killing me." Connor groaned and pressed his hips forward until he hovered at the entrance to paradise.

She held him tightly and didn't let him enter.

"Please tell me you didn't change your mind," he begged.

"Please tell me you have a condom," she countered, her brow furrowed and her face desperate.

Shit, he'd almost forgotten. Fortunately old habits, leftover from his time in the Army, were hard to break and he'd loaded up his pockets with a variety of emergency supplies this morning before he came to work. Although he would never have predicted he'd be using this particular supply. "Left leg. Second pocket down."

Conner let Ava delve into his pocket while he slicked his fingers over her swollen and plump sex. She moaned as she ripped the wrapper open. He continued to play with her clit and rub his fingers in the sweet juice that coated her sex. She was so fucking ready and he couldn't wait to bury himself deep inside her. He tilted Ava's hips up and spread her wide for his invasion. She fell back on the desk, her knees up by her chest. Connor threaded his fingers through hers and pressed her flat against the fancy cordovan leather desktop. She lay before him like a feast.

Her face was flushed, her lips roughened from their frantic kisses, her sex spread wide open and waiting for his invasion. His arms were hooked under her thighs as he paused at her entrance. Connor rubbed the head of his cock along her slick folds and moaned as the heat of her pussy beckoned.

"Quit teasing and do it," she growled. Shit, that take charge voice turned him on. She was usually so damn quiet. The fact that she got bossy during sex really did it for him.

With one desperate lunge, he thrust inside her.

Con paused, held clasped inside her velvet fist, as he absorbed the sensation of coming home. Which was ridiculous of course. She wasn't home. She was just a hot woman with an itch. A hot woman he'd been quietly observing and lusting after for months while he ignored his building desire. But the ache in his chest grew as he slowly slid out until his tip teased her clit, then he slipped back inside her.

Ava's eyes fluttered closed as she lay like a goddess opened purely for his pleasure. And only his. The weird and uncomfortable feelings spread over him blanketing his passion in some otherworldly sensation.

Which was ridiculous.

This was just sex.

With that thought, he slammed back inside her slick channel. Ava grunted. At first he thought he'd hurt her, until she demanded, "Again."

Con stared into the mysterious depths of her dark eyes as he plunged inside her. She stared right back keeping them connected, and that sense of coming home speared through him with lightning force.

Con powered in and out of Ava. She lifted her hips to meet each thrust with abandon. Her breasts bounced each time they came together and Ava was making little erotic noises as her body tightened around his. He could feel the muscles of her sex gripping him with a fierce intensity. His orgasm gathered at the base of his spine, as his cock hardened even further and he felt as if he didn't let go soon, the top of his head would blow off.

*MADRE DE DIOS*. Connor hit every erogenous zone she'd ever had or thought she had. With every slam, the head of his cock massaged her g-spot, the root rubbed her clit, and with each hard foray his cock head hit her cervix. She was overwhelmed, over-stimulated, her body shaking with the need to come.

Suddenly he swelled impossibly larger until she thought she was being rent in two by the erotic intrusion of his hard, thick length.

His fingers tightened on hers, and with a hoarse shout he spurt inside her. The force of his orgasm triggered hers and Ava bowed up from the desk as her womb contracted almost painfully around his throbbing cock. Stars exploded behind her closed eyelids, and her limbs trembled forcefully as she came long and hard.

Connor continued to thrust in and out, his orgasm battered her sensitive walls and triggered another mini climax. Her head swam as she was bombarded by sensory details. The hairy roughness of his thighs against the back of hers, the way she was spread wide against the invasion of his hips, the hot wet suction of his mouth as he bowed over her and lapped at her over-sensitized nipple.

Ava jerked at the sensual contact and her womb contracted again and again. Her orgasm seemed to last forever.

Connor kissed a path up the center of her breastbone where her heart beat frenetically. He was still buried balls deep in her, his heart thud against her chest, his pectorals pressed against her breasts. He brushed a tender kiss across her lips.

For some reason, the sweet gesture made her want to cry.

When was the last time she'd been touched with tenderness by a lover? Never. With all the inherent affection of his soft gesture, he'd touched some soft spot deep inside her that longed for the affection of a man.

Her former attempts at sex had been fumbled, furtive

encounters in messy apartments and cluttered dorm rooms. Not impersonal but she'd never really connected with her partner. Not the way she'd wanted to.

But was this any better?

She felt connected but that feeling was a lie brought on by endorphins and the lingering euphoria from an epic orgasm. As far as she knew, before today he'd barely even noticed her. So whatever weird connection she thought she felt, it was all in her head. A ridiculous fantasy she'd nurtured over the last year. Yearning from behind her desk as he went about his days never really seeing her.

The sensual cocoon that surrounded them was ripped apart by her doubts, and reality hit her in the face. She was lying on top of her boss's desk, for God's sake. Her running shorts were wrapped around one ankle and she still had her Nike running shoes on. Connor's pants hadn't made it any further down than his thighs. A deep mortified flush spread throughout her.

What had she just done?

Con was wrecked.

He slumped over Ava, completely undone by their explosive sex. His heart thudded painfully in his chest as he took stock. His pants were barely mid-thigh. His t-shirt and her shirt were somewhere behind him—probably on the floor. As he looked down at Ava sprawled over Jack's desk, a grin spread over his face.

Jack was going to be sorry he'd said anything.

She stiffened beneath him.

"I'm not laughing at you," Connor said quickly. Shit. He didn't want her upset. But her face settled into an unhappy mask.

Trying to placate her, he seriously put his foot in it. "I was laughing at Jack."

Her entire body froze.

That just made it worse. "Crap. That didn't come out right."

"*Madre de Dios.*" Her deep black eyes widened, framed by thick black lashes and shimmering with an abundance of regret. Ava shoved at his shoulders. "We've got to...." As if she finally realized that the seal was broken and protesting was futile, she slumped back down on the desk and covered her face with her forearm.

"What have I done?" came out muffled and just the slightest bit panicked.

"Come on now, it isn't that bad."

"Not for you. You won't lose your job over this."

A shamed sensation spread through him as her words registered. Would he ever fucking live down his behavior from his past? He couldn't even get away from his former reputation with a woman who hadn't known him then. Connor straightened, pulled his cock from her clearly now unwilling body. He disposed of the condom in the wastebasket under the desk.

"That's what you think of me?" Connor jerked his pants up with an angry yank. "Nice."

"No. I don't know." Ava crossed her arms over her chest, hiding her breasts from him. She flushed a deep red, and awkwardly twirled her hand. "Could you...."

"I've already seen your charms," he said snidely as he zipped his pants and then reached for her spandex running top. He tossed it to her without meeting her gaze. What had he done in the past year that would make her think that he would get her fired? The ache in his chest intensified.

So much for that sense of coming home. If this was home, he was getting kicked to the curb before he could get comfortable. Like always.

"I'm sorry." She said miserably, "It's just...I love this job."

"I know. And fuck you very much for thinking I would even consider jeopardizing that."

Ava dressed frantically, but she didn't say another word. She tugged her shorts up and adjusted her breasts as misery spread through her. She was clearly incapable of saying the right thing.

She twisted, trying to straighten the shelf bra in her top and put herself back together. As she turned back around, she bumped the old-fashioned black phone that sat next to the blotter.

Ava's breath caught in her chest. She'd clearly hurt his feelings. Which seemed odd and surprising. In all her fantasies she hadn't ever once considered that he had feelings. He was always so controlled and calm. With his mussed hair and rumpled t-shirt clutched in his fist, he looked nothing like his normal, relaxed, composed self. His face was a mask of stillness but underneath that blank facade he was upset. And she was the one who upset him.

The temptation to soothe him was strong but Ava couldn't dwell on that right now. "We have a problem."

"I'd say we have more than one."

Ava was trying to smooth her hair into something that didn't look like she'd just had sex on her boss's desk. But really what was the point? "Riley never checked in."

"Fuck." Connor threaded his fingers through his hair and tugged. His bicep bulged and the muscles in his six-pack rippled. "What the hell is going on?" he whispered.

Guilt crossed his face before he turned away from her. The muscles in his back tensed and turned to stone as he tugged his t-shirt over his head.

Con faced the window overlooking the Pacific Ocean. The sun had long since set, and the moon had risen early so that shadows and light rippled over the myriad of waves. So great, while he was getting it on with a woman who clearly had a really shitty opinion of him, his brother Riley was out there, somewhere in the Philippines and had missed his check-in. One miss wasn't the end of the world, but taken

with everything else going on, Con struggled not to worry. And he needed to figure out what the hell was happening on every front.

Another wave of guilt rolled over him. Jack had entrusted GHR and Stone Consulting to him just this morning and since then things had literally started going to hell. He'd managed to fuck everything up. *Way to prove yourself, Con.*

"Are you okay?" Ava's fingertips brushed tentatively across his tense, tight delts.

"Just great," he lied. He wished she'd just...leave.

"Umm, is there anything I can do to help?"

"No, go on home." Con rubbed his hand through his overly long blond hair. Since he'd left the army he'd let it grow. Now it flopped over his forehead and curled around his ears.

"Oh, okay."

He could see her reflection in the large picture window. The glass was coated with a reflective covering so that they could see out but no one could see in, which was good, otherwise someone would have gotten quite the show with his bare ass hanging out and her running shoes digging into his butt as he'd pounded in and out of her.

Her hand hovered over his shoulder, as if she wanted to comfort him or touch him again. But he didn't touch people and people didn't touch him. He was far more comfortable around computers and motherboards. A fact very distinctly driven home by the fact that she thought he was the kind of guy who would get her fired for having sex with him.

Yeah, touching people didn't seem to go all that well for Con.

"By the way, if anyone loses their job, it will be me." Con huffed out a mirthless laugh.

"What?"

*Way to go, Con.* He mentally patted himself on the back. His first real chance to prove to Jack that he was responsible, that he belonged. And he'd blown it. Deeds not words. The company had been hacked. Riley had missed his check-in. Jack's assistant had been followed. And Con had jumped said assistant on Jack's very sturdy desk.

He hadn't done anything to stop the first three, and actively participated in the last one.

Deeds.

He needed to get his head back into whatever was happening at the company and get it out of fucking Ava Sanchez. Literally. "Never mind."

She rubbed her fingers over her biceps as if warding off a chill. Her eyebrows quirked in a tiny frown that disappeared before Con could even register that she was worried about something. Her job. She was worried about her job.

"I promise you won't lose your job."

"What?" she blinked absently as if her thoughts were on another continent. "Oh, I believe you."

"Okay. Good. Fine."

But if she believed him then what was bothering her?

"Do you need anything else from me tonight?" Her tone was polite, distant. Ava had her head turned slightly to the side, gaze averted as if they hadn't just done the nasty in Jack's office, on Jack's desk. Back to the way she'd treated him in the past. Looking at him without quite looking at him.

"No. We're good." Con went through what Jack had requested of him. Which meant taking control of everything out of control. He could spend the night here and continue to try to trace the hack. Riley was next on the list. "Are you supposed to be here for another check-in with Riley?"

She paled. "I have to come back tomorrow at the same time."

"Is there a backup time if he misses check-in number one?"

"No." She still wasn't looking at him. Awesome.

Con thought about what Riley was doing in the Philippines. Delivering books and school supplies in the Sulu Province on the island of Sulu near Jolo. An area known for harboring MNLF, the Moro National Liberation Front, rebels. On the surface, his mission was humanitarian and feel good. But Con assumed there was more to Riley's trip than philanthropy. Currently there was a peace accord in place, but what if the government was looking for extra information on the MNLF to make sure they were on board with the treaty and really willing to maintain peace?

Could the rebels, or terrorists depending on your viewpoint, have caught on to Riley's other purpose on the island?

"What protocol is in place if he misses another one?"

"First miss is a warning." Ava shook her head, her ebony hair curled around her face, swung against her soft, rounded cheek, and a single strand caught on her mouth. Con battled the urge to brush the silky black lock away with his thumb and then follow it up with his mouth.

Shit. She'd distracted him again. Of course, it was all his fault. Maybe he wasn't as reformed as he thought.

"Second miss puts the company on standby," Ava said slowly.

Standby. Con wondered if he needed to contact Shane and make sure he could be available with minimum notice. Shane. He needed to try to call Shane and Jack again.

"Third miss triggers a company extraction," Ava finished. "Of course, no one's ever missed three check-ins. At least, not since I've been here."

Extraction. Con mentally started compiling lists of what he'd need if Riley and his counterpart from *Tools for Schools* needed rescuing. Con wouldn't be able to do it alone. His stomach curdled at the possibility that he'd need to ask Jess for help. He'd do it. Deeds not words. Con strengthened his resolve. "Okay. Don't worry about it. I'll be here for tomorrow's check-in."

"But—"

"See you next week." Connor interrupted. "Have a nice Thanksgiving." He forced the impersonal words out through stiff lips and shoved down his awkward feelings. "Let me walk you to your car."

"No thanks," Ava replied. She held her body tight as she grabbed her purse and the hanging bag with her suit, her sexy pumps dangling from the opening at the top.

Remorse hit him hard.

He didn't want her to leave this way. Everything about the last few hours was crazy, impulsive, and intense.

He got that she was done with him, but he wasn't going to let her walk to her car in the dark. Monterey wasn't exactly a hotbed of crime. And for a former soldier, the crime here was no problem. However, Shelley had raised him right and there was no way he was letting Ava walk to her car alone.

Since she had refused his offer, Con followed quietly behind her. He'd make sure she got in her car safely and then he'd go back to work. See if there were any way to trace the breach and continue to dig deeper on José Fernandez.

Ava took the stairs down to the underground parking

garage and Con followed silently behind her. When she reached the landing, she whirled around and crouched into a fighting stance. She relaxed as she realized it was only Con and shot him a dark look without verbally acknowledging his presence.

Ava continued down the stairs. If body language could talk, she was saying: asshole. Except after the slightest of pauses, her shoulders softened and her hands unclenched. He realized that she'd been tense and worried until she discovered that he had her back.

Con stood in the half-open door to the parking garage and conscientiously watched her walk to her car.

Her running shoes made little sound, only a slight swish and the minute squeak of her left shoe on the slick concrete floor as she strode to an older model Honda Civic that had seen better days. Con leaned against the door frame and listened to the slight shush of her legs against each other and the muted rush of cars on the road above them. They were the only ones in the parking garage this late on a Friday.

She was almost to her car when Con registered another sound in the garage. The slight scuff of a hard heel was distinct in the sequestered silence. Then Con saw the man moving stealthily toward Ava. Con was blocked by the door, so he didn't think the guy had seen him yet. With only a moment to react, Con began to run.

AVA FELT a whoosh of air behind her and whirled around to confront Connor. "Will you stop—"

Sheer terror caromed through her. It wasn't Connor. A man, clothed all in black with a nude-colored ski mask over his face, rushed her.

Ava screamed, dropped her stuff, leaned back on her left leg and kicked out with her right. All those sessions with a trainer paid off and she managed to get a few debilitating kicks and blows in.

But then the man dodged her kick, wrapped his arms around her and shoved a cloth against her nose. "*Buenos noches, puta,*" he growled and those were the last words she registered as a sickly, sweet smell overpowered her.

## CHAPTER 7

onnor's heart literally skipped a beat when he saw Ava slump in her attacker's arms. He pumped his arms and sprinted toward them. He cursed the fact that he'd already locked his weapon in his office safe, although even if he'd had it, he couldn't risk shooting for fear he'd hit Ava.

A car screeched around the corner and stopped in front of the pair.

Connor put on a burst of speed. No way was he going to let them get Ava into that car. In a split second, he assessed his options. Slide across the hood then be impeded by driver's door or run around the rear of the car and hope he could get there before they could finish getting Ava into the backseat.

As the driver gunned the engine, Connor made his decision and raced toward the open back door.

The first guy was trying desperately to get Ava in the back seat of the car, but he was hampered by the dead weight of her body.

*Fuck!* Connor prayed that she was only knocked out, not actually dead. Otherwise why take her?

*Thug one* was bent over Ava and halfway into the car with his back unprotected. Con punched her kidnapper in the kidney with three sharp jabs. The guy whirled around too quickly and had to overcorrect. Con shot a one-two punch at the guy's jaw, and his head snapped back as he staggered against the open car door. Con undercut into a large but hard belly while the guy feebly tried to protect his body.

The driver, *thug two*, had turned around to see what the problem was. Con split his attention between the two kidnappers. *Thug two's* eyes were wild behind the nude ski mask as he gunned the engine. But he didn't take off. Thank God. Because even though Ava's torso lay safely on the back seat, her legs still hung outside the car.

*Thug one* took a swing at him. Con arched away from the blow, his focus splintered between *thug one* and *thug two* trying to intuit their plan. The open rear passenger door effectively hamstrung the driver. But Con was more worried the driver would change his mind and take off with Ava half in, half out of the car.

Con's main objective was to rescue Ava.

His heartbeat slowed, and the *thud-thud* echoed in his brain. The harsh rasp of his breath reverberated in his skull. His vision tunneled as he took in details. The engine gunned again. *Thug one* lunged at him and he knew had no choice but to unleash the fury boiling within him. With a fierce desperation, Connor pummeled the attacker in a barrage of blows grunting at the force of his rage. No one was going to hurt Ava on his watch.

Finally the asshole dropped to his knees and fell to the side. Con scooped up Ava and ran for her car. His souped up Dodge Charger was too far away. She'd already unlocked the Civic, so he yanked open the passenger seat and tossed her in carefully, all the while trying to keep focus on her assailants. Luckily Ava carried her keys on a sparkly lanyard around her neck. He lifted the lanyard over her head and slammed the passenger door shut.

Connor raced around to the driver's seat. As much as he'd like to capture these guys and beat answers out of them, his number one priority was Ava.

Con slid into the driver's seat and assessed her. She appeared to be asleep, her chest rose and fell in deep, easy breaths. So Con turned his attention to the assailants. His brain processed information, noting that the old boat of Lincoln Continental was minus license plates. Although both thugs wore ski masks, their hands identified them as one Caucasian and one darker skin, could be Hispanic, Middle Eastern, or mixed blood. Likely not African-American.

While Con had been getting Ava in her car, *thug two* had rushed from the driver's seat and shoved his partner into the backseat and threw himself back into the car. The Lincoln shot forward on a burst of speed.

He didn't want to leave Ava alone on the bizarre off chance they had another partner. But he could follow the old Lincoln.

Con gunned the Honda's engine, completely exasperated when her little car barely turned over. He shifted to drive. The car rumbled and coughed as he gave the engine more gas but the car chugged forward sluggishly. He desperately watched her assailants' car, powered by a V8, shoot away in the rear-view mirror. He tried one more time to get the Honda to go faster than twenty miles an hour but the damn thing felt permanently stuck in first gear.

"Dammit." Con rested his forehead on the steering wheel and took a moment.

He shifted into Park and leaned over to check on Ava.

Her head lolled against the passenger window as she sagged limply against the car door. Her chest continued to rise and fall slowly. He lifted her eyelid and peered at her pupils which contracted slightly.

Punching numbers into his cell, Con dialed with one hand while he measured the slow, easy beat of her pulse. When Amir, his doctor, answered he got right to the point. "If a woman is drugged—" Con sniffed and was pretty sure he detected the sweet scent of chloroform. "—with chloroform, how long will she stay unconscious?"

"You do know there isn't any legal limitation on doctor patient privilege. In a court of law, I'd have to testify against you." Con could practically see his pal smirking.

"Jokes later." Con held Ava up against the worn passenger seat with one palm. "I'm serious."

Amir quieted down and asked a series of questions. "Breathing?"

"Easy."

"Nausea?"

"She's not throwing up or looking like she's going to throw up."

"Color?"

"Color?" Con frowned. "What?"

"It can affect the liver," Amir snapped.

"Oh. Rosy cheeks and lips." Con looked at her heart-stoppingly beautiful face. "She just looks like she's asleep."

"Try to wake her up."

Con glanced back out the garage exit. The kidnappers were long gone. Now he had to concentrate on Ava. He patted her cheek lightly. "Ava, sweetheart. Wake up."

Nothing.

He patted her cheek a little harder, wincing at the sharp sound of the slaps. "Ava."

She lolled her head to the side and squinted her eyes open. Her mouth curved wide and her tongue slicked across her lips as he cupped her jaw in his palm to hold her head steady.

"*Ho-la hombre guapo*," she slurred as her lids drooped closed again. Then she barely whispered, "*Usted es muy caliente. Usted me hace mareado.*"

Amir snickered on the other end of the phone. "Let her sleep. Unless she starts having problems breathing, she should be fine. And it's likely the chloroform making her dizzy, not you, hottie."

Con ignored Amir's teasing. "You sure she'll be okay?"

"Just let her sleep it off. She'll wake up when her body has equalized the drug, and she'll probably feel like she's got a hangover."

Con jabbed the end button on his phone. The band of worry around his heart eased and he breathed a relieved sigh. He pulled the seat belt over her prone form and buckled her in. "Safety first," he murmured. Then he asked the unconscious woman, "Who wants you?"

*Besides me.* The thought popped into his brain. He smoothed her hair away from her face and frowned at the dark bruise forming on her cheek. He pressed a soft, gentle kiss to her skin and then headed toward the only safe place he could take her while he figured out what to do next.

Home.

A DULL THUD persisted in knocking against Ava's skull like the boom of a wrecking ball. Her tongue felt about ten sizes too big for her mouth and her sealed lips cracked when she tried to separate them. As she attempted to swallow a sharp, thick pain hurt her throat.

*Dios*, she had the worst hangover in the history of time.

Her eyelids were crusted shut and through sheer force of will, Ava finally pried them open. Watery light filtered through her vision. Sheer filmy curtains she didn't recognize hung in front of her and blocked her vision of what lay beyond the bed. She'd been a little disappointed when she'd left the office but she didn't remember going on a bender. She wasn't a drinker except for a *cerveza* on hot summer nights and the occasional glass of champagne for special events. And she didn't remember anything special happening last night. So why was she in a strange bed? Her heart kicked. Why didn't she remember? The harder she tried, the more her head hurt.

She frowned and took stock as other details shimmered in her foggy, sluggish mind. The inferno of heat that emanated from behind her. The heavy weight across the curve of her waist, and the gentle, unexpected cocoon that sheltered her and protected her. She felt so safe.

The steady rise and fall of the chest behind her. The thick column of thighs that spooned her legs. The insistent throb of the erection pressed into her butt. Except, she had never in her life slept with a man.

She was fully dressed. In her workout clothes. Somewhat tight and uncomfortable, spandex wasn't the best sleepwear.

She jerked in surprise when all the details came together and coalesced into a coherent picture. A distinctive, masculine scent drifted over her senses and she identified the man behind her. Connor Stone? She was in bed with Connor Stone. Panic, insistent and urgent, caromed through her. How had she ended up in bed with *Connor*?

As if attuned to the slightest change in her body, Connor

stiffened against her back and his arms tensed then squeezed lightly before he let her go. He carefully rolled her around to face him. "How are you feeling?" he tenderly brushed a lock of hair from her face and frowned at something he saw.

Apparently, she'd been drop-kicked into some alternate universe where her fantasies were reality. She was in bed with Connor Stone.

"Connor?" Her voice was raspy as if she'd been asleep for a thousand years instead of.... Why couldn't she remember?

"You okay?" Connor asked.

But she didn't answer, trying to process.

"Nothing?" As if he had read her blank mind and understood her memory was completely *unclear*.

The last coherent memory she had was of them on Jack's desk. She flushed, a deep full body blush that started at her toes and tingled through her until her face was as red and as hot as a habanero chili.

Connor threaded his fingers through hers, his palm hard and calloused against her much smaller one. His chest was bare, and he wore a pair of plaid flannel drawstring bottoms that hung low enough on his hips that his exquisitely-defined inguinal muscles were exposed.

His chest was a sculpted work of art with thick deltoids and pecs that tapered down to a his rippled abs. His skin was marred with dings and a few older scars, battle wounds that she was sure would make her flinch if she knew exactly how he received them.

Heat surrounded her emanating from his body like the sun on a hot summer's day. How could she even focus on what he was asking? All she could think about was the notion that he'd reached right into her deepest, darkest, most hidden fantasies and given them to her.

She clenched her fist against the desire to smooth her hands over his naked skin and curl her fingers around the bulge she could clearly see beneath his pants. All the yearning she'd hidden behind downcast eyes and furtive glances rose to the surface as if he had turned over her fallow field and exposed the roots of her attraction. If she dared to look into his hypnotic eyes would she see desire or disgust? Either answer terrified her.

Ava refused to look at him and he let her get away with it.

"You were attacked, drugged."

A hazy memory of Connor running at her full bore as an overly sweet odor invaded her senses surfaced.

"Do you remember anything?"

"No. Not really." She swallowed and licked her lips. "Why am I here?"

"It was the only safe place I could bring you."

"Where exactly am I?"

"My family's house."

She shot straight up in bed and finally looked at him. "Your mother's house?"

"Technically, she's my stepmother but yes."

Ava got caught by the odd inflection in his voice. Why did he have that little catch when he'd mentioned his stepmother? But then the more important fact registered. She was in bed with him in his family home. And as much as waking up with him next to her was at the top of her fantasy meter, doing so in his family's house was not.

"What did you do?" She tried to disengage their fingers, but she couldn't because Connor held tight. "Why am I in bed with you in your mother's house?" her voice rose as the full implications hit her.

"I needed to keep an eye on you until you regained

consciousness," Connor said patiently, calmly. He spoke to her like her family when they talked to her ancient *Tia Lucia*, who couldn't hear well and thus had trouble understanding simple conversations.

She had to get out of here. She was scrabbling at the covers with her feet and trying desperately to disconnect their fingers. "Well, consciousness regained so *adios*."

# CHAPTER 8

*I*t didn't take a genius, which he was, to figure out she was upset. But Con didn't understand why. He was more charmed as he noticed that her accent was all but eradicated unless she was upset or aroused. And the heated look in her dark eyes, before they'd started discussing exactly where they were, told him she might be a little bit of both.

She was going to hurt herself if she kicked much more and Con couldn't stand for that to happen. He drew her up against his chest and whispered in her ear, "Shh. I'm not going to let anyone hurt you."

She balled up her fist and punched him in the stomach but the hit lacked intensity because of the proximity of their bodies. "You, *imbécil*. I can't be in your bed in your family home."

"Technically it's not *my* bed. We're in the guest room." Con's mouth quirked as he nuzzled the sweet spot behind her ear and slid one hand to curve over her butt. "You didn't hurt your hand, did you?"

"What?" She drew back and for a second, she looked so

angry, Con thought she might head butt him. "Can you focus on the bigger issue here?"

Even more important than the 'bigger issue' was the fact that she was looking him in the eye again. "I am. The bigger issue is who is after you. You aren't going anywhere until we figure that out."

He swallowed his worry. He'd spent the last few hours digging deeper into José Fernandez. But the guy was clear as crystal. He had done everything to make sure his actions were never construed any way other than straightforward and noble. While Fernandez had personally advanced his political star during the search for the abducted girls, he never profited from the situation in any other way. Everything he'd done had brought good things to the migrant community.

Many of his friends and constituents regarded him as a hero.

Even though Jack and Ava didn't have a good feeling about him, Con could not find anything nefarious or wrong with his past and nothing to implicate him in Stone Consulting's current problems.

The only other thing Con had done was call his sister. He'd come to the conclusion that he couldn't tackle the current situation with the company alone if Riley missed check-in number two. He needed her here and ready to take on an extraction.

"We don't need to do it from bed," Ava cried.

Con couldn't stop the swell of gratitude that rolled over him. She was safe.

But as she tried to get up and away from him, the move thrust her breasts into his bare chest. Connor groaned at the unexpected contact. He also noticed that she was clearly aroused as the hard points of her nipples brushed against him. He insinuated his leg between her thighs and went light-headed at the heat from her sex. She was saying one thing, but her body was telling a completely different story.

A visceral thrill ran through him. She was as helpless in the grasp of their sexual attraction as he was. Her breathy sigh blew across his forehead. She had her head tilted back on the pristine white cotton sheets and the long column of her neck was exposed to his gaze. With unerring accuracy, his attention narrowed on the rapid flutter of her pulse in the hollow of her throat.

His own heart picked up rhythm as his body responded to hers. And the longing that had struck him last night when he'd held her in his arms, rescued her from the attack, and protected her from the threat against her, came back in triple force.

The need to touch her, hold her, confirm that she was safe and whole and *here*, slammed into him. What would have happened if he hadn't followed her to the garage? What would have happened if her abductors had been able to get her into the car before Con had gotten to her?

Instead of bringing those worries up, he asked what he really wanted to know. "Would being in my bed be so bad?"

She stilled and her deep black eyes widened. "Of course not." She shifted in the sheets, her body a hairsbreadth away from his and yet, she was so distant she might as well have been across the room in the chaise lounge at the window. "But what will your mother, stepmother," she corrected before he could. "Think?"

She would be thrilled that Con had finally brought someone home. But Con couldn't say that. He couldn't reveal how big a deal it was that he'd brought Ava here or she'd be out of the house faster than he could say, "It's not what you think." And that was unacceptable. Someone had

wanted her badly enough to drug her and attempt to kidnap her in a public garage. No way in hell was he letting her leave this house without him.

Nothing he said was going to put her at ease. Her lashes lay dark and thick against her bruised cheekbone. Connor couldn't resist the lure of that hurt and he brushed a gentle kiss against the obscene purple blemish even as he cursed the fact that he hadn't gotten to her in time.

"I'm just happy you're okay," he whispered in her ear.

"You...saved me." Her eyes blinked open. "I—I'm starting to remember."

Con's pulse quickened. Maybe she could give him more information. "What do you remember?" Maybe they could catch the fuckers who hurt her. "Did they speak? Say anything?"

"No. He just grabbed me."

He remembered with sickening detail how the guy had jammed that cloth over her nose and she'd sagged in his arms. His stomach cramped.

"Damn, Ava. I saw him drug you but I couldn't get there in time," he said. "Swear to God, my heart nearly stopped." He curled his arms around her and tightened his grip as if unwilling to let anyone get near her again.

"Connor." She brushed the hair from his face tenderly. Her body melted against his, her soft to his hard, tightly clenched muscles. "You rescued me."

"I won't let anyone hurt you ever again," he said fiercely. "That's a promise."

They needed to get out of this bed before Con did something he'd regret. Something like roll her over and make sweet love to her. He'd already broken that rule and the aftermath hadn't gone so well. Not to mention that Ava had to be traumatized by the events of last night.

"I thought my self-defense class had taught me the right moves," she said. She hunched shoulders rounded and head down.

"Let me show you some other moves." Connor figured it would serve two purposes. One, to help Ava learn to defeat her attacker next time, God forbid, and two, it would get them out of this bed. "You can practice beating me up."

She straightened and a brilliant smile lit her face. Her mouth curved and the downcast expression disappeared in a wave of delight. "Yes please."

Con wasn't sure she needed to be so happy about beating him up, but he preferred happy rather than worried or embarrassed. Con vaulted out of the bed. He gestured to Ava in a 'come here' taunt with his fingers. Ava gingerly slid off the bed. Then he looked at her, really looked at her. She was a vision with her hair tousled and her eyes heavy-lidded as she swept the last of sleep away with a lazy rub of her fingers.

Ava yawned, with her mouth wide open and her head tilted back in abandon, she stretched her toned sleek arms over her head and her breasts shifted beneath the constricting spandex top. Con thought about all the other things they could be doing in a bedroom rather than working on self-defense. His cock, which had seriously deflated after their talk about her attack, stirred to life.

"Turn around," he said gruffly. "I'm going to approach you from behind."

Ava obediently twirled around so that her back was to him and her front faced the tall four-poster bed. Con took a deep breath, willed his cock to settle down, and started instructing her on how to break the hold of attacker from behind.

But he realized he had made a serious mistake the

second he put one arm around her waist and the other around her neck.

The sweet valley of her cleavage was in his direct line of sight. And even as he sidestepped her attempt to stomp on his instep instinctively, his palm slid up the side of her ribcage until he nearly cupped her breast in his hand.

He needed to concentrate on trying to attack her. If she went for a groin shot, she was in for a big surprise. Connor was harder than the pine posts of the canopy bed. Ava executed a few more self-defense moves that were pretty good.

"You've got the hang of this."

"I studied self-defense." She panted.

"But you forgot it all when you were attacked?" Connor shifted again, trying to approach her from a different angle.

"No. I was *éstupida*. I let my guard down because I thought you were following me. I assumed it was you."

Connor heart stuttered at the realization that he'd contributed to her attack, even if it was a misunderstanding. He tightened his arms around her waist, unwilling to let her turn around. He didn't want to see the accusation in her deep black gaze. She kept saying she didn't blame him but how could she not? The only way to atone was to teach her something new. "Never let your guard down."

She gripped his wrists with surprisingly strong fingers and peeled his arms from her body. Before he could step away, Ava whirled around. "It was not your fault."

"I certainly didn't prevent it." He shifted his attention to the fluttering sheer panels that surrounded the bed.

Ava placed her soft palm against his cheek and turned his head so that he faced her fully. "Connor, you saved me," she said fiercely.

"Maybe." He shrugged.

She stepped into his space, went up on her tiptoes, and pressed her lips to his. The contact was sweet, cool, as she initiated their kiss.

Connor stepped into the kiss, giving in to the temptation to touch her, to take solace from her forgiveness.

"Why are you beating yourself up?" she murmured against his mouth.

Why was he? Because she meant something to him. And the idea that she was almost taken, was assuredly hurt, even though he had rescued her, cut deep. He finally acknowledged that he had feelings for Ava beyond the lust he'd suppressed over the last few months.

For the past year, she'd quietly, sweetly smiled at him. Accepted him for who he was now, not some younger more immature, more reckless version of himself. She never saw that guy. The one he was always trying to live down. At least not until last night.

He thought about her confessions in Jack's office.

She saw *him*. Just like he saw her.

On a visceral level that defied logic and defied the depth of their interactions before this weekend, he saw her. But Con had a feeling if he admitted that she'd take off faster than he could say, *Stay*. He needed to show her how he felt.

Deeds not words.

So he kissed her. He poured every bit of gratitude and relief that she was okay into the kiss. Con cupped her face in his hands and scattered kisses across her face, touching on her cheekbones, the tip of her nose, the shell of her ear, the sensitive spot below. Each caress was a gesture of thanks. Of relief that she had not come to any harm.

Fuck it. The bed was right there. She wanted him as much as he wanted her. Con nipped at her lower lip then sipped his way into her mouth. He licked at her lips and wooed her with kisses until she sank against him, her once stiff body soft with surrender. Her breasts pillowed onto his chest and his erection rubbed along the V in her legs.

He planned to ask her permission. But before he could separate his mouth from hers, she shoved him onto the bed and climbed over top of him.

He broke away from the kiss. "Jesus, that is hot." Her natural aggression during physical intimacy was an incredible turn on. She was normally so quiet. Until she saw something she wanted. Or he pissed her off.

As he lifted his hips to nudge her with his sex, she spread her legs wider. The sweet kiss he had initiated turned feral and crazy hot. Connor reveled in her female curves as he slid one hand down to cup her ass. He rocked her hips against his and swallowed her breathy moan. Her hands explored his chest, running her fingertips along his skin like a blind woman reading braille. He worshipped her with his hands, embracing her curvy body with reverence, as if he could hold her, protect her forever. Because that's what he wanted. Forever.

He wanted this thing between them to be a beginning, not just a response to danger and an adrenaline let down from a perilous situation. But they barely knew each other. She had no reason to trust him. Con wanted to give her every reason to trust him, to turn to him.

Ava sank on top of Connor. His erection bulged beneath the soft flannel, and the sight of him caused everything within her to soften as her body prepared for his. All the reasons why this was another bad idea flit through her mind as she rubbed against him.

But the one reason to keep going trumped every other reason to stop. He had saved her. As if the universe was telling her to seize the day, she surrendered to the arousal thrumming through her. Her limbs were lax and her body languid as he rolled again until she was beneath him. She was in bed with Connor Stone, and based on the erection prodding her belly, he wanted her. She might not get a chance like this again.

He held her tight, his arms curled under her shoulders and his legs between hers. The feeling so right she lost her breath.

"I'm glad you're okay," he said.

"Me too," she replied breathily. She'd cheated fate once more.

After Maria disappeared, she'd made a promise to herself to live life to the fullest. Living life right now meant seizing this moment. Seizing *him*.

His face was half in shadow, the dappled light from the wall of windows highlighted his sharp cheek bones and his blond-stubbled jaw. His longer hair fell over his eyebrow and shielded his gaze. He looked scruffy, something she'd never seen before, and unbearably sexy. Usually Connor was very tidy and clean-shaven. The beginnings of a beard gave him a more rakish air. The soft hair abraded her chin as he sipped at her mouth. Her skin tingled with each sweep of his hand.

The Stone brothers were notorious as the subject of office gossip.

According to the legends, of which there were many, Jack and Riley had voracious appetites. But what about Connor? Could she keep up with him?

She was damn well going to try.

Ava ran her palms over the warm skin of his chest and marveled at his sculpted, lean muscle mass. His biceps bulged as he propped his upper body over her and kept her ensconced within the protective custody of arms ropy with thick dark veins. As she stared into his eyes, the tawny brown and gold blazed with heat.

For her.

She may not be the most adventurous woman on the peninsula but what she lacked in experience she planned to make up for with enthusiasm. Ava licked her way up the thick column of Con's neck and smiled as he shuddered at the contact. Her hands slid over the defined muscles of his back and toyed with the loose waist of his flannel bottoms.

His erection prodded her as he grew harder.

Connor shoved up the tight tank of her workout top and cupped her breast in his large, calloused palm. His hot mouth closed over her nipple and she involuntarily squeezed his ass.

He smiled against her breast. "I'm guessing you liked that."

So now Mr. Silent had decided to get talkative?

She liked that he talked to her. Con tended to be a watcher. An observer who contributed when asked but didn't run his mouth. Ava liked that he wasn't silent with her, that he wanted to talk to her.

Ava panted as his mouth created a sizzle from the tip of his tongue down to her sex. Her body buzzed and fizzed as he kissed his way across her chest and made love to her breasts as if he'd been stranded in the desert for the last ten years.

Her head was floating, and she was desperate for him. Frustration clawed at her. If he didn't get inside her soon, she would dissolve into a giant puff of air. And never be seen again.

"So I hear you think I am *muy caliente*," Connor murmured against her breast.

"What?" she almost banged into his head as her chin

came up and her entire body blushed. How did he know that?

"Apparently you get a little...loose-lipped while under the influence of chloroform."

"*Madre de Dios.*"

She'd told him she thought he was hot? What else had she said? And did she even want to know?

Ava was determined to make him forget anything she'd said while drugged. What if she'd told him about her fantasies? About her daydreams?

Con laughed, his teeth white and even as he bent and nipped at her mouth. "I think you're *muy caliente* too."

Just like that he washed away her embarrassment. Ava shoved at his flannel bottoms, even as Connor ripped her top over her head. She cupped his ass in her hands, marveled at the heat of his erection prodding her sex.

As if that final confession lifted a barrier from their desires, they frantically tore their clothes off. Within seconds, they were both naked. The power and heat of his body enveloped hers. He was so big he made her feel petite.

Connor quickly grabbed a condom from a drawer in the bedside table. Ava skimmed her hands over his powerful chest as he propped up on one elbow and rolled the protection over his cock.

His extremely large cock. How had she missed that yesterday? "You're huge."

Connor laughed softly. "What every man wants to hear."

"*Si* but not what every man is."

Connor rubbed the head of his cock along her swollen aroused sex. The contact was firm, but he didn't enter her. Ava curled her fingers around his hips and tried to take control. Silently demanding that he come inside her.

But Connor held back, rocked his hips. Each time he slid just a little further inside her. Her sex clenched, begging for his deep invasion. "Now," she demanded.

He thrust inside in one long deep glide and held there. The root of his cock pressed against her clitoris, as her slick channel swallowed the thick broad length of him.

Ava moaned, the sensual invasion so sweet and so right. Her heart pounded and her pulse thudded. With a little whimper she rocked her hips silently begging for him to move.

"Dammit, Ava." Connor bowed over her and pressed a sweet kiss to her lips. "I wanted to be gentle."

"Screw gentle." She panted. "Next time."

With her words a giant smile spread over his face, lightened his somber gaze. With a wicked grin he began to move.

Connor slid his palms beneath her butt and yanked her to him. They were connected at every touchpoint, mouths, his thick chest against her breasts, their groins locked together, and their legs entwined.

Connor pulled all the way out until only the head of his cock nudged her clit.

Then without warning he plunged inside.

*Yes.* Each slam blasted her erogenous zones, her g-spot, her clit, every nerve in her sex was massaged and aroused by his powerful movements. Connor surrounded her, enveloped her, overwhelmed her body and mind with the power of his thrusts.

Every cell in her body rejoiced at the intimate connection. Flames of desire roared through her body as her soft yielded to his hard. Her blood pooled and sizzled. With one urgent final thrust, Connor froze in a rictus of release. His groan reverberated through her body and the hard, fierce pulse of his orgasm triggered her release.

Her womb contracted around him each tight pull of her muscles created ripples of aftershocks throughout her body. Every nerve was over-sensitized as she experienced a nearly euphoric high.

She'd never come so hard in her life.

Her chest and throat were so tight, she couldn't speak. Shouldn't speak because all the fierce emotions bombarding her would likely come tumbling out in some sex-induced confession and she'd never live it down. So instead she pressed kisses along his shoulder and neck. His face was buried in the curve of her shoulder, his hair tickled her ear and the heavy press of his body felt incredible.

She could stay like this forever.

JESUS. Con was wrecked. Again.

He wasn't sure he could move, let alone speak. The power of his orgasm had rendered him deaf, dumb and nearly blind.

He sank into the sweet cradle of her body and hoped he wasn't crushing her. He'd move in a second. Speak in a second.

Right now, he had to get his thundering heart under control and his thoughts ordered before he opened his mouth and blurted out something crazy, like, *come live with me.*

But fuck him, she'd done it again. She felt like home. Like shelter. Like acceptance. And Con was starving for the opportunity to have this every day. To feel like this every day.

Three sharp knocks sounded on the thick wooden door. Distantly Con registered the sound but it took a moment to process because all his blood had recently drained from his head and he was still recovering from a massive orgasm.

The distinctive click of the lock shifted everything into clarity and before he could do more than roll over and yank the sheet up over their bodies to protect Ava from his stepmother's gaze, she had opened the door and called out gaily, "Knock, knock. Oh! Oh, my."

Connor hadn't been caught in this position since he was eighteen.

"Well, I'll just...go on back downstairs." Shelley faltered, then powered through the rest of her announcement as if she hadn't just caught them in the act. "Lunch is ready when you are."

"*Madre de Dios,*" Ava muttered against his neck. "I am going to hell."

Connor snorted. "I don't think it's quite that bad."

"Easy for you to say." She bit him hard. And just like that his cock, which had wilted slightly at Shelley's interruption, surged back to life.

"Well then I'm going with you," he teased. "Come on. We'd better get to lunch."

"I can't meet your stepmother now," she wailed.

"Technically, you already met."

# CHAPTER 9

*Ava* shifted on the rough-planked bench seat at the Stone's kitchen table. The long table was constructed of wide oak boards, stained in a dark finish with enough room to seat eight adults. The kitchen was huge. Almost as big as her entire apartment, the room boasted a wall of white cabinets with glass fronts, gray granite counters with gold and bronze flecks that gleamed, and a backsplash in rustic glass tiles of varying metallic shades. Three funky teardrop lights hung over an island big enough for four wood bar stools.

A large mahogany bowl polished to a high shine overflowed with mini-pumpkins, gourds, and dried corn. The placemats were a deep burnt orange with mustard yellow trim.

Connor's stepmother served lunch, massive BLT sandwiches and apple cobbler, on brown square plates that matched the tabletop perfectly.

It was like stepping into a magazine cover shoot.

Condensation trailed down the side of her tall glass of iced tea and reminded Ava why they were late. She flushed.

"So nice to finally meet you." Connor's stepmother, Shelley, smiled and brushed an affectionate hand over Connor's shoulder. For all that Connor felt necessary to clarify that Shelley was his stepmother, she clearly loved her stepson and didn't necessarily feel the same distance he did. Shelley appeared to touch him freely with a sweet, motherly smile on her face. Although she didn't appear old enough to be Connor's mother, more like his older sister.

"Nice to meet you too," Ava replied huskily. She cleared her throat and willed her body to stop flushing, still embarrassed by the fact that Shelley had seen them in bed. Although it had been painfully obvious what they had been doing, thanks to Con's quick thinking, Shelley hadn't seen them naked. But it had been close.

Ava took a large gulp of iced tea. The frigid liquid soothed her abused, dry throat. Feeling ridiculously parched, she slugged down most of the cool drink and avoided conversation. She shifted her attention to the large picture window and almost choked on the tea.

The Pacific Ocean crashed on the uneven rocks a hundred yards from their back door. It was one of those gray foggy afternoons, where the marine layer clouds hovered over the ocean like a foreman over the field workers. Giant redwoods flanked their property and created a secluded grove which hid the estate from the prying eyes of the tourists who paid to drive along Seventeen Mile Drive.

Off to the left was a large swimming pool, surrounded by rocks similar to the coastline, and which sported a waterfall that recycled water back into the pool. Encircled by various trees and foliage, the habitat made it seem as if the pool were actually a natural pond. An expanse of green grass led to the tumble of rocks at the edge of the ocean, scattered with a few straggling cypress trees. Some weathered branches that had broken off from the trees were strewn across the rocks creating an artistic backdrop for the crashing waves.

The back door was open, ushering in a brisk salt-scented breeze and the bark of the seals on the rock formation out in the swirling eddy of their inlet.

*Santa Madre de Dios.* She'd known the Stone family had money. But they had *money.* "You grew up here?" she blurted before thinking. Ava slapped her hand over her mouth and closed her eyes in mortification. "Oh, *lo siento.* Very rude."

To stop from saying anything else embarrassing, she shoved the bacon, lettuce, and tomato sandwich in her mouth and took a big bite. Ava nearly moaned. It was so good. She flushed again and wondered if she could make any worse of an impression.

Shelley's laugh trilled softly. "The view gorgeous, isn't it? I never get tired of it." She propped her chin in her hand and stared out the large window. "I still remember the first time I saw the ocean. I was awestruck. Remember, Con?"

Connor shifted on his heavy wood chair. "Um, yeah. Of course."

Connor had gotten very quiet and Ava wondered what he was thinking. He looked pensive and slightly uncomfortable.

"You were such an adorable, quiet little guy," Shelley said softly.

Connor appeared to blush but didn't say a word.

"Not much has changed." Shelley cleared her plate from the table and carried it to the large farm sink. "I've got to run to Watsonville. I'm volunteering at the food bank this afternoon. Ava, honey, stay as long as you need to. Con filled me in last night. You need to be safe," she rambled on as she loaded the dishwasher. "And we have plenty of room."

"Thank you," Ava replied. She had to admit that going home to her lonely little Victorian apartment didn't hold much appeal. She thanked goodness that her parents were in Sinaloa visiting relatives, they would be freaking out at the fact that she'd nearly been abducted. Although she worried about them there, they were probably safer in Mexico right now.

"Con, be a sweetie and start the dishwasher when you're done." She bent over and brushed a kiss against his cheek. Ava couldn't help but notice that he tensed up a bit. "You did good bringing her here, honey."

But the thought was swept away as Shelley patted Ava on the head and then rushed out the kitchen in a whirlwind.

Ava sat at the table somewhat stunned by the force of nature that was Connor's stepmother. "When did Shelley and Jessica come to live here?"

Con watched Shelley go then twisted back to face Ava. Twenty years later, his stepmother never failed to give him some affection and it still threw him. She'd blown into his life at eight and made him her own. He might always be out of step with his siblings but Shelley never let him get away with that with her.

Even in his rebellious teen years, when he had acted out against Little Miss Perfection, Jessica, who got good grades, never came home drunk, and could do no wrong, Shelley gave him unconditional love. Con did everything he could to live down to his father's expectations until Shelley set him on the right path. He owed her everything, but he still had trouble with her easy affection. And he never forgot that she was not his real mother.

He'd realized after talking to Jess on the phone last night that he needed to clear the air with his sister. It wasn't her fault that their father was an ass. It wasn't her fault that with his long blond hair and weird tawny eyes, he looked unlike any of his siblings or his father. Just one more way he didn't fit in. His brothers used to tease him that he was probably adopted but everyone knew Jack Senior had paternity tests done every single time some new kid popped up. And every time they'd come back positive, including Con's, because dear old dad was a complete man whore.

So when Jess and Shelley had come to live with them, suddenly there was a face for all of his feelings of being an outsider, and he'd rebelled against being perfect like Jess. But he was an adult now, and Jess's surprise when he'd called to ask for help had been crystal clear even through the transatlantic connection.

Con shook off the memories. He needed to focus on here and now. Ava was still waiting. What had she asked? Oh, yeah. "I was eight."

"Did your dad get remarried?" Ava asked curiously.

He'd never been married to Con's mother. His mother had dropped him at Jack Stone Senior's, taken a lump sum payment, and hit the road. Con didn't even remember her. He'd been dropped off to live with Jack and Riley and their dad when he was a baby. The only reason he knew exactly what happened was Jack Senior made sure to give him a callous recitation of the truth when he'd been five and thrown a temper tantrum when he didn't get what he wanted.

And his dad may have devastated him with the circumstances of how he'd ended up with him and his brothers, but Con had also learned then that bad behavior got him noticed. Even if it wasn't quite the attention he'd wanted.

Ava seemed to be calculating something in her head and then she blurted out, "You and Jess are only three months apart."

"I am aware."

She opened and closed her sultry mouth a few times. "So...."

"Dear old dad was screwing my mother and Shelley at the same time."

"Connor!"

"My father couldn't keep it in his pants." Con stood abruptly and stalked to the sink. He dumped his tea down the drain and put the empty glass in the dishwasher. "Still can't for that matter."

"Does he live here too?"

Con snorted. "No. Thank God."

Their family dynamics were messed up enough that it would take a flow chart to figure everything out. Con couldn't be sure but he thought his father might have finally stopped spreading his sperm around and gotten a vasectomy a few years back. "Horny bastard," he gutted out.

"You shouldn't call your father—" Ava scrunched her eyes closed. "Wait, he said something."

Con stopped. "Who?"

"The guy who grabbed me."

"What did he say?" Con wanted to nail these guys. He balled his fists on his hips and waited impatiently for her to share. He forced himself to sit back down at the table and let her remember.

Ava was swamped by his navy sweats and an old Army t-shirt. She looked adorable in his clothes, and he couldn't help but feel proprietary as he watched her move. Her full breasts filled out the worn t-shirt nicely and he was thankful that she hadn't had a choice of attire. Because Ava wouldn't fit in Jess's clothes—she had too many curves, in all the right places as far as Con was concerned—she'd had to borrow some of his.

"He called me a *puta*."

Slut. "Why would he call you that?" Con got up and began to pace the Saltillo tiles. "You're about as far from a slut as a nun." Connor's shoulders tightened and he bulked up as if getting ready to face an enemy. No one called his girl a slut.

*His girl?* He mentally jerked back. Whoa. She wasn't his. But he'd like her to be, the thought wound through his mind like a wisp of fog that slithered along the ground in the early morning.

Ava blinked, lowered her lashes and averted her gaze. "If they saw me on Jack's desk yesterday, they might have had reason."

Con stalked to the table so quickly, Ava's head jerked up. He gripped her delicate shoulders, her muscles tense and bunched beneath his fingers. "No way. That wasn't—"

But she interrupted him, clearly not wanting to discuss their interlude on the desk. "He was probably just mad that I got in a few good shots before he could get the cloth over my face. Instinct."

So Con let it drop and concentrated on her revelation. The guy had used one accented Spanish word. Just like Ava when she got upset, little hints of her accent would come out. "So at least one of your attackers was Hispanic."

"I still don't understand why they would want me." A frown puckered her elegantly- shaped brows.

Con didn't like the theory that was forming in the back of his mind. So he looked for anything that might dispute his uncomfortable conclusion. "Any unusual behavior lately?"

She shook her head mutely.

"Any other feelings of being followed?" He knew he had been right not to dismiss her concerns after she felt like she'd been followed on the beach.

Again, a negative answer.

"Take up any hobbies lately. Start doing something new?"

"No, no, and no. All I do is work and work out," she said glumly.

He didn't know why she looked quite so down. "Me too."

If it wasn't about her personally, then it would make sense that it had something to do with GHR and Stone Consulting. "Have you done anything differently at work lately?"

Her eyebrows rose. And she spoke without thinking, "The only new thing I've done is you."

Con stifled a laugh and pressed a quick hard kiss on her lips.

But that niggling sensation that he got when he was debugging code wouldn't let him go. He hated the connections his brain had made without even trying to connect the events. But he sensed he was on the right track. Ava was the link between the kidnappings eight years ago and Stone Consulting's investigation into José Fernandez now.

What if Fernandez thought that Ava knew something about whatever happened to those girls? What if he knew that Stone Consulting was investigating him? Or what if Fernandez realized that Stone Consulting was investigating him and he thought Ava would be the weak link? It became even more crucial than ever for Con to find out what Fernandez was hiding.

"What?" Ava's fingers were curled around Con's wrists as if she didn't want to let him go. Con normally didn't like being touched but with her he craved every stroke of affection she was willing to give.

Con only had his own suspicions and it was a long shot. But his brain kept going there. He hesitated. Jack had asked him not to tell anyone what he was working on. But Ava wasn't anyone. She was his. And she had a right to know what he thought. "Before Jack left, he asked me to investigate José Fernandez."

"Fernandez?" she grimaced again. "Why?"

Jack was gone. He'd left Con in charge. He had two goals now. One, to keep Stone Consulting and GHR exactly the way Jack left it. Two, protect Ava.

But that order was wrong. Ava came before the company.

"I don't know. He just wanted everything and anything I could get on the guy." Con wished he'd found something glaring in the check he'd already done but whatever Fernandez was hiding, it had to be buried deep. "It was a Stone Consulting job, not GHR." Revealing that difference was not something that necessarily sat well with him but this was Ava. And he trusted her.

"While I don't know everything that the company is involved in, I'm not an idiot." Ava traced the woven circles of the placemat with her finger. "You think the Fernandez job has something to do with me?"

"Someone obviously wants something from you. If Fernandez knows you work for us, and if he thinks you know something about the disappearances of those girls then maybe. Yes."

"You think Fernandez was behind the kidnappings?" she said incredulously. "I mean, I don't like the man but that's a pretty big leap."

"You are the only connection between the two events."

Con watched her process his suspicions. Watched her brain make the same lightning conclusion that he had.

"If that's true...." she trailed off. Her elegant fingers had covered her mouth in distress.

"We have an opportunity." Connor didn't candy-coat the truth or try to hide his suspicions. She was a big girl. She could handle whatever he threw at her, so he put his idea out there. "If Fernandez was behind your kidnapping, then we could flush him out."

Right now they had nothing. Just three isolated events and one single, very thin denominator. The fact that one of her attackers, may or may not be Hispanic was hardly a strong enough connection to take to the police and definitely not the kind of intelligence that Jack was looking for. But....

"Bait," she whispered.

"Yeah." If they could draw Fernandez out, they might get evidence that would incriminate him.

"No."

Con's shoulders sank. He couldn't say he was fond of the idea of putting her in potential harms' way. On the other hand, they had nothing concrete. But he certainly didn't blame her for refusing. "Okay."

"I don't want to dangle out there waiting for him to come to me or go after me." Ava fisted her hands on her hips, her black eyes sparkled with anger. "I want to confront him. I want you to control the situation."

"What?" Connor just barely stopped himself from reaching for her again.

"Forget waiting for him to come after me again." Ava jabbed her finger at Con. "Let's go after him."

"Ava," Con started. His heart expanded, swelling in his chest at her expression of trust. And that's when he fell. His heart had teetered at her sweet confession when she'd been only half conscious. But her fierce need to expose the truth and her insistence to be proactive instead of passive caused him to tumble the rest of the way in love with her.

Ava placed her hand over Con's clenched fist. "I mean it." Her touch soothed him and excited him. People didn't touch Con. He knew it was his own back off vibe that sent the 'do not touch' message. But Ava bulldozed right over it and stoked the fire higher. She ignored the signals and went with her gut.

"If he had something to do with those girls' abductions…my *friends*," she said fiercely. "Then I have a responsibility to make sure everyone knows about it."

Con could hardly argue with her. He understood about making up for the past. He understood about atoning for prior sins. "Ava, you know there was nothing you could have done."

"I know that now." Ava quietly confessed, "But it didn't stop me from feeling guilty all those years ago."

"You were a kid."

"Old enough to be working in the fields." The downturn of her plump mouth distracted him for a second. The urge to crowd her up against the table and kiss her senseless was strong.

"Now if I have the chance to find out, to do something to expose his sins and I don't take it, *that* would be my fault."

Con acquiesced. There was only one response to her resolution. Con laced his fingers with hers, marveled at the sheer softness of her skin. Marveled at her fierce devotion to her friends, and her willingness to get to the truth.

"You're sure?"

"Yes." She squeezed his fingers with hers.

"I will keep you safe."

She brushed her lips over their clenched fingers. "I have no doubts."

$\mathcal{A}$va inhaled deeply, slowly through her nose, focused her thoughts and wished she'd paid more attention in the one yoga class she'd taken. She needed to find a calm center.

She wanted to do this. She *did*. But that didn't mean that she wasn't scared out of her mind. Worst case, Fernandez had nothing to do with her friends' disappearance or her attempted kidnapping, and she would make a complete fool out of herself by making the accusation. Best case, Fernandez was in it up to his eyeballs and she would be instrumental in helping expose him. Maybe finally there would be some justice for Maria and those other girls.

Connor kept crowded to her right side. Ava swallowed when she noticed that attached to his belt was a holster that held a big, black gun. The presence of the weapon ramped up her anxiety rather than reassured her.

Connor noticed her gaze linger on his weapon. "Don't worry. I'm a marksman."

It took Ava a moment to compute his words. He thought

she was worried about her safety. "I know you can defend us. I don't want you to get hurt."

"That's...nice." One corner of Connor's mouth curled up in a half-smile. With his left hand, he smoothed his thumb across her cheekbone. "I'll protect you."

"I never had any doubt."

The surprise in his tawny eyes hit her like a punch to the heart. She knew that his family cared about him, it was evident in the way they interacted with each other. Easy banter and subtle digs, but always delivered with a smile, as if everything they did and said was an inside joke. But Ava had seen the shadows in Connor's eyes. Recognized the way he held himself back from his brothers and with Jess. But he didn't hold back with her.

So how could Connor think for a moment that Ava wouldn't trust him to take care of her? Her heart stalled at the vulnerability she'd glimpsed, and she vowed to make sure that Connor knew how much she trusted him. "I would never have suggested this if I didn't have absolute faith in your ability to keep me safe," she said the words like a vow.

It was time to confront Fernandez on his own turf. His own very public turf.

José Fernandez was considered a pillar of the community. Nothing would happen to her while she was in his office. And if Ava repeated that thought to herself silently over and over maybe she could make the belief true.

Jess had returned from England early. Much to Ava's surprise, Connor had called her late last night and she'd caught the first plane home to help out. So she was backing up their little mission.

Jess was ensconced on the rooftop across the street from the office. Her rifle was assembled and ready but more importantly, her weapon of choice this afternoon was a high-powered camera she had trained on the interior of Fernandez's storefront office.

Before she could chicken out, Ava brushed a kiss over his lips, initiating the sweet contact. "For luck."

Connor curled his arm around her waist and yanked her body flush with his. He slanted his head and covered her mouth in a possessive, demanding kiss. She melted against his hard body as she savored the public show of affection and let hope blossom.

Maybe, just maybe, he was as swept away as she was by the allure between them that flared, bright and hot.

"Okay you two, let's get this show on the road." Jess's voice sounded in her ear, and Ava heard the underlying affection.

A thrill swept through her as she noted that he'd kissed her back, even knowing that his sister was tracking them through the lens of her camera.

"They'll have to go through me to get to you," he said fiercely. "That's a promise."

Before she could tell him that she didn't want anyone else's hurt on her conscience, Con checked their surroundings. He opened the door to Fernandez's office with his left hand, his right resting loosely on the hilt of his gun. They walked in together, Connor slightly in front of her, not completely blocking her but covering her body with his.

The office was small but tastefully decorated. Couldn't be too fancy seeing as the constituents who got him into power were frequently new immigrants, factory workers, and field workers. He'd built his entire reputation and platform on helping underserved and marginalized citizens.

His receptionist was equally tasteful, dressed in a tailored cotton blouse and skirt. She wore a simple gold ring on her ring finger. "Can I help you?" the receptionist said congenially. A light coat of makeup evened out her features and gave her face a healthy glow.

"We'd like to see Representative Fernandez," Connor replied equally as pleasantly.

"Do you have an appointment?"

"We don't. But I believe he'll want to see us," Connor continued, still in that weirdly friendly voice. "We'd like to discuss a charity with him."

The receptionist blinked her tastefully-shadowed eyes and said slowly, "Okay. Can I have your names?"

Connor gave their names and the receptionist had them wait while she got on the phone.

Within a few minutes, she hung up and smiled at them uncertainly. "If you can wait a few more minutes, Representative Fernandez always has time for his constituents." But the furrow between her eyebrows was deep. She had no idea why Fernandez was willing to see them without an appointment.

"Great. Thanks," Con replied.

He made sure Ava stayed on his left side and kept his weapon hand free. The odds of Fernandez attacking them here were slim but Con refused to let down his guard while he was responsible for Ava.

And he kept their positions such that Jess could get every moment of this confrontation on film. About twenty minutes later, Fernandez came out to the reception area.

He had that slick look that all politicians perfected. His Hispanic heritage was only slightly evident in the smooth black hair, gently graying at the sideburns, and dark unreadable eyes. But his suit screamed inside the Beltway and his face was buffed and polished. Clearly, he'd shaken off the roots that had gotten him where he was today.

Funny but the last time Con had seen Fernandez on

television, at a new after-school rec center in the middle of a mostly immigrant community, he'd been wearing jeans and a plaid shirt. He guessed that didn't play as well with the Washington crowd.

"Thanks for seeing us without an appointment." Con kept his voice light.

"Always happy to chat with my constituents." Fernandez smiled wide, his capped teeth, white and even. His handshake was firm, short with the perfect grip. Not too tight, not too limp, no clammy skin, and no nervous tremble. "What can I do for you folks?"

Con understood why Ava and Jack had a weird feeling about the guy. He looked right. He smiled right. He said the right things. He was *too* right. No rough edge, no glimmer of sincerity.

"My name is Ava Sanchez," Ava inserted smoothly. "I work for GHR. Global Humanitarian Relief. A local private relief organization. We supplement the efforts of relief agencies in addition to spearheading our own relief and philanthropic efforts."

Ava sounded perfect. Like she was in PR for the company and seeking support instead of searching for information into Fernandez's shady activities.

"Nice," Con murmured.

"It sounds like a wonderfully helpful company." But there'd been a flicker of worry as his eyelids flinched subtly.

"We've chosen to put our efforts toward a new organization, S.S.A.F.E.," Ava continued with her information spiel, trying subtly to take Fernandez off guard. "Have you heard of it?"

"I can't say that I'm familiar with the organization." The guy's veneer didn't slip at all. If anything, his smile got more smarmy. "If you want my support, give the literature to my assistant, and I'll have my staff do some research."

But Ava ignored his brush off. "S.S.A.F.E. stands for Security, Shelter, and Freedom for the Exploited. The organization helps abducted and trafficked women reintegrate into society after they are rescued."

"It sounds like a very worthy cause." Fernandez crinkled his brow convincingly and he'd subtly relaxed.

"I would think you'd be interested in supporting the cause since the disappearance of the girls eight years ago very positively impacted your career," Ava said sweetly. "There's a good chance those girls were trafficked."

There was no change in his outward demeanor, but Con swore Fernandez was suddenly paying a lot more attention. "It was a great tragedy."

"Your career benefited immensely from the kidnapping of those girls."

"Now, Miss Sanchez." His smarmy smile dimmed. "I can't believe you would even think such a thing."

Ava refused to back down. This guy had made his career on the most devastating, life-changing tragedy of her life. "Maria Torres was my best friend."

For a mere second, Fernandez's smile slipped, and Con swore he could see into the reptilian soul that lived beneath that slick exterior.

"I'm so sorry for your loss," Fernandez intoned insincerely.

Chances are the girls were gone but suddenly a thought occurred to Con. "No bodies were ever found."

Fernandez's mouth turned down. "You're right," he murmured. "Still after all these years it would be a miracle if the girls were still alive."

Something about that statement hit another chord in

Con's consciousness. No bodies were ever found. He thought about Jack's cryptic message to someone, somewhere in Washington. What if the proof, the *evidence*, was a person? What if someone had discovered those girls were alive and where they were?

His heart quickened. It would be a miracle.

"Let's pray for a miracle then," Con said softly.

That's when he saw the minute crack in Fernandez's armor. He knew something or he had a guilty conscience.

Ava saw the crack as well. As if the knowledge unleashed her inner warrior she got right in Fernandez's face, stepping into his personal space, shooting accusations at him. "Did you have something to do with their disappearance?"

Fernandez's smile didn't waver. A concerned frown barely rippled the smooth line of his forehead. "I'm sorry, *mi joya*, I thought you were here to discuss the new project for GHR. Not rehash old news."

"I am not your jewel," Ava snarled. "Those girls that you built your career on...did you have something to do with their disappearance?"

"My dear, are you completely delusional?" Fernandez kept up the pleasant confusion. He'd clearly perfected the benign puzzled expression.

"You getting this?" Con asked softly, connecting with Jess who was across the street and three stories up. The tiny transmitter buttons they wore had hyper-sensitive mikes that were able to pick up quite a bit of background sound as well as the voices of anyone speaking within ten feet of the mike. They'd hopefully be able to hear what the receptionist was saying as she spoke into the phone handset at her mouth.

"Affirmative." Jess's soft laugh was like music. "You've managed to give him a slight tick."

Con assessed Fernandez and sure enough his left eye twitched slightly.

"Good going." Jess laughed again.

Ava fumed beside him, temper burning in her gorgeous black eyes. He didn't think she should have brought up the attack so soon, but he also understood Ava's need to confront Fernandez and maybe get answers. The disappearance of those girls had haunted her and shaped her choices from fifteen until now. Ava's hands were clenched into fists at her side and she leaned in further. "I'm watching you."

Fernandez's smile slipped just enough that Con knew they were right. But he hadn't said a word that confirmed their suspicions and they still had no proof that Fernandez was guilty. They barely even had speculation. The connections were so thin a soft breeze would tear through them. "I would never hurt anyone. What could I possibly have had to do with the abduction of your friends? But even so, it is not smart to threaten an elected official."

Con's stress level went through the roof. This guy was trying to intimidate Ava.

He bulked up his shoulders and stepped closer to Ava and by association Fernandez.

Even if the Stone family hadn't had any personal interactions with Fernandez a smart politician knew every wealthy connected potential donor in his jurisdiction. And pissing off a Stone sibling was not a smart move.

"But I am a man of the people, and I know I must always make time for everyone," Fernandez said softly. "Even if they are not quite right."

Con felt the presence of security guards at his back. Fernandez shook his head negatively, quietly directing the guards not to accost them which was smart. Evicting constituents tended to make you look guilty even if you could prove you were innocently accused.

Con thought it might be good to get a look at the men. Surely Fernandez wouldn't use his own security team to try to kidnap Ava, but he had to rule them out. Con turned around slowly and assessed the men. Their body types were all wrong and clearly not a match for Ava's abductors.

"I think our work here is done," Con said softly.

"But—"

"Later, sweetheart." Con curled his left palm around Ava's bicep and tugged her toward the door. Con tipped an imaginary hat at both Fernandez and the bodyguards who hovered menacingly close to where the three of them stood.

"Thanks for your time," Con said to Fernandez. And then let him know that they had pictures of the meeting. "I'm sure we'll be seeing you real soon. But just in case we'll be sure to send you some commemorative photos of this meeting."

He hoped that this meeting had effectively prohibited Fernandez from going after Ava again. And just maybe this little visit would shake something loose if they had rattled Fernandez enough.

*"Para curar no basta la intencio,"* Fernandez said softly, his gaze firmly trained on Ava. He ignored Con, recognizing that Ava was the more volatile of the pair.

Ava whitened but whatever the words meant she didn't back down. She leaned forward pressing into Fernandez's personal space again. "They will never be forgotten. *Que nunca serán olvidados,*" she said fiercely.

"I hope you get the help you need." Fernandez reached out his hand. Con could see the slight tremble in his fingers as he patted Ava on the hand. José Fernandez issued the warning softly and it sounded like a threat. "You should be thankful that you weren't taken."

"Don't touch her," Con growled. Something about Fernandez's demeanor set off every hot button he'd ever had. "Don't come near her ever again."

He'd put his hand on his weapon to punctuate his warning.

Fernandez reared back.

Con's phone rang just as cops came screeching into the parking lot, sirens blaring. *So that's who the receptionist had been on the phone with.*

Con's phone continued to ring. He lifted his hand from his weapon and grabbed his phone. It was Jack. Shit, he had to answer. Con pressed the Talk button.

"Con?" Jack barked.

"Jack, now really isn't a good time."

The cops scrambled out of their car.

"Ava is in danger," Jack spit out.

"Jess get down here now," Con commanded, then addressed Jack. "I know. I was trying to fix it."

"I'm worried she's going to be abducted," Jack continued.

Con's chest swelled. "I stopped it."

"Thank God." Jack's voice was full of relief.

But the full extent of Con's actions just became clear as the cops raced to the doorway of the office. Con was fucked.

He'd saved Ava. But he may have just destroyed GHR's name. The shit storm from a company employee threatening an elected official was about as far from keeping the company safe and taking care of business as possible. And Con knew he'd royally fucked up.

"But Jack," Con continued as the cops burst through the front door. "I'm about to mess up GHR's good name."

"Ava's safe?"

"You aren't listening to me. I fucked up and GHR is going to be all over the news."

"Ava's okay? You're okay?" Jack clarified.

"Yes." Except for the fact that he was likely going to get arrested in a minute.

"Thank you, Con, I'm proud of you. You did good."

Happiness at Jack's praise ballooned in his chest filling him with pride. He'd finally lived down the bad memories. He was amazed he could be so thrilled and so filled with remorse at the same time. Because the cops were closing in.

Con heard a woman on the other end of the line. "Who are you talking to?"

"Shit," Jack blurted out. "Got to run."

The woman's' voice rose. "Get off that phone now. You're going to ruin—"

The line went dead just as the cops drew their weapons. "Hands in the air."

Con lifted his hands, laced his fingers and placed them behind his head. "Hello officers." He smiled his best 'I'm harmless' smile. Unfortunately when he'd put his hands behind his head, his jacket had lifted up and his holster and weapon were clearly on display.

"On the ground now."

"Jess. Take care of Ava," Connor ground out as he sank to his knees and carefully lay face down on the ground.

"You can't arrest him," Ava protested.

Jess pushed open the door to the storefront, her camera slung around her neck and no weapons in sight. Jess curled her fingers around Ava's bicep. "Come on. Let's get out of here."

"We can't leave him!" Ava's voice rose.

"Ava, hush." Con turned his head so he could see Ava

and Jess. "I'll be fine. You guys head to the station in case I need to be bailed out."

The cops had relieved him of his weapon. "I have a permit to carry concealed," he said to the linoleum floor.

"We need to check it out," one of the cops said as he cuffed Con's wrists together behind his back.

"I don't want to leave you." Ava was tugging against Jess's hold. She wasn't crying. She was pissed. "Why are you arresting him?"

"Assault."

"That's bull. He didn't assault anyone."

"Who knew our sweet little receptionist had it in her?" Jess snickered and the sound reverberated into his earpiece.

"That's my girl," Con said softly.

Ava's startled gaze shot to his, her dark black eyes rounded and wide-eyed with surprise.

"Really?" Jess said speculatively.

"Yep."

"Really?" Ava had stopped struggling with Jess.

"You're mine," Con said fiercely.

Fernandez looked confused. Ava looked shocked. And Jess continued to chuckle in Con's ear.

"Take care of her," Connor directed.

"I can take care of myself," Ava countered.

As the cops lifted him to his feet, his hands were cuffed behind his back, his shoulders bunched awkwardly beneath his jacket.

"We're going to take you to the station," the second cop said.

"Now, let's just everyone calm down," Fernandez interjected.

It occurred to Con that Fernandez wasn't going to want a record of this altercation. Maybe he hadn't completely messed this up. Con raised an eyebrow. "But don't you want to press charges?"

The cops shot him a funny look.

"I think an apology would be just fine," Fernandez spoke in his smooth politician's voice.

"You sure you don't want a record?" Con smiled.

"Most people would be happy to avoid booking and the court time pal," the first cop said.

Con turned to the second cop. "Does this call stay on the books with the witnesses and participants," he shot a glance at Ava. "Named and documented whether charges are pressed or not?"

"Yes. Since dispatch registered the call, paperwork will have to be filed," the second cop said slowly.

"Let's not be too hasty." Fernandez smiled the smarmy smile. "I don't want to get anyone in trouble."

The receptionist blanched.

"You do what you have to do officers." Con relaxed his shoulders, smirked and waited to be taken downtown or let go. Either way this whole altercation would be on record and Ava would be doubly protected. No way Fernandez would try anything against her now.

"No charges?" the second cop asked Fernandez.

"No. I can understand the heat of the moment." Fernandez deflected. "Everyone makes mistakes."

"That would be most...understanding of you," Jess said.

Ava didn't say a word.

"And who would you be?" Fernandez had lost his politician's demeanor and had started to fray around the edges.

Jess held out her hand. "Jessica Stone. I voted for you."

Fernandez whitened visibly as his gaze shot to the

camera dangling around Jess's neck. Oh yeah, he knew where she'd been, and he knew they had pictures.

He swallowed. "Thank you for you vote."

"We still need to follow up here." The first cop lead Con to the bank of chairs along the wall. "Even if no one wants to press charges."

"Is that really necessary?" Fernandez's smile was strained.

"Yes." The police set each of them down in the reception area and interviewed them individually. Ava carefully explained why they had come to visit Representative Fernandez, avoiding the accusations that she'd spouted earlier and focusing on the information regarding S.S.A.F.E.

"It's a charity that garners a lot of passion," Fernandez said smoothly, his mask firmly back in place. "No one could blame her for getting heated about the subject."

Ava smiled tensely but managed to keep her mouth shut. Thank God.

But when the cops asked what lead to the escalation, everyone glossed over the exchange that culminated in Con touching his weapon. When they were all done, the police released Connor from the cuffs and thanked him for his cooperation.

The Stone family name had done a lot to smooth over the situation.

They left the office and headed to Jess's Jeep parked a block away.

Connor gave Jess a hug. A long one.

"What was that for?" Jess lifted her brows at him.

"Thanks for having my back."

"Any time."

Con tried to tell her without words how sorry he was for

all the times he blamed her for his issues. "Same goes. You know that, right?"

"Umm."

Deeds not words. Con hugged her again then stepped back. Jess smiled at him and then said, "Looks like we both had some growing up to do."

"We need to talk," Connor said to Jess. They needed to go over what to do next. And what to do about Riley's lack of communication and Jack's lack of information.

"Could one of you drop me at home?" Ava asked.

Con was speechless. She thought she was going home? Not a chance in hell. He realized that Ava hadn't said much since his declaration that she was his. He was pretty sure he understood exactly why. He'd scared her.

His. She was his. And he was hers. He got that. Even if she wasn't sure yet. He knew that she just needed time to get used to the idea. To allow herself to be happy. And Con was going to make sure she was happy.

But he also needed to take control of what was happening with GHR and Stone Consulting. He'd promised Jack.

And that was when he realized exactly how he would get Ava to stay with him.

"I got a ping on the breach in our system." He'd had the alert sent to his phone. To complicate things, the breach was coming from Monterey. From their office.

"That's great," Ava said. "So we've got them?"

"Not quite yet."

"Why not?"

"Because it came from your computer's IP address."

"What?" Ava shook her head.

Jess jerked in surprise.

"But I didn't…you have to know…." The panic on her

face stopped him. Shit. He totally hadn't thought this through.

"I know." Con wanted to grab her and reassure her. "Jesus, of course you didn't."

She blinked. "Then how?"

"That's what we need to figure out." Con couldn't stand it any longer. He threaded his fingers through hers. "But I need you…to come back to the office. We need you with us so we can figure out how they managed to infiltrate our system."

Which was a total lie. He could figure it out on his own, but he wasn't letting her out of his sight.

# CHAPTER 11

"Let me just go upload these pictures into our system." Jess lifted the camera from around her neck and headed to her office. "Then I'll be right back."

They had come back to GHR's headquarters together since it was almost time for Riley's check-in. Jess had done an SDR and no one had followed them. Of course, Fernandez had to be sweating right about now.

Ava sat at her desk with her palms pressed flat on the surface. "You have to know that I didn't—"

"No question in my mind."

Her shoulders slumped. "Thank you."

"But they did somehow get into our system. Maybe some sort of phishing email."

Ava jerked. "Like a blank email?"

"That would do it if you clicked on it."

"I did. I was distracted." She flushed and then fluttered her hands in distress. "I already deleted the email."

Con finessed the keys on her keyboard, hyper aware of

the heat of Ava's body next to his. "Found it. I'll see if I can follow the trail back to whoever sent this."

He set up another backtrace and then turned to face her.

She was so damn beautiful.

"Ava—"

"Pictures should be loaded onto the system in a few minutes. In the meantime, we can…."

His sister had the worst timing.

"Oh, I can go," Jess said.

As much as he wanted to claim Ava for his own, he didn't want an audience. And he didn't want to be rushed. Besides, Jack had put his trust in Con and he didn't want to let him down.

"We need to get this done." He looked at Ava. "Give us a few minutes and then we can do a de-brief on the situation and compare our notes on the altercation with Fernandez."

She nodded, not meeting his gaze.

Con and Jess sat in the more casual grouping of leather chairs in Jack's office. Con figured there was no time like the present to clear the air.

"Thanks for having my back." Con said softly, "And looking out for Ava."

"No problem." Jess smiled, her green eyes sparkling.

Con had figured out that if he wanted to move forward, he needed to get this out. "I've been doing a lot of thinking lately—"

"You didn't hurt yourself, did you?" Jess joked.

"Ha. Ha." In the past her teasing would have raised his defenses. "Seriously, Jess, I'm sorry about your friend, Laura…." Con trailed off. He couldn't for the life of him remember the girl's last name. Wow. He'd gotten drunk and seduced his sister's best friend and thrown the entire house into chaos and now he had no idea what her name was.

Jess stretched her legs out in front of her and slid down so that she slumped in the chair. "Con, seriously?"

"I fucked up."

"She was only my friend because she wanted you," Jess revealed with a roll of her eyes.

Well that was a new take on it.

"But I got her drunk—"

"She got herself drunk." Jess shook her head. "I realized long before that night that she had an agenda when it came to you. Sure, you came home drunk, but she'd already stolen a bottle of mom's vodka and put it in a water bottle when I'd changed into my pajamas."

"But you were pissed."

"At *her*."

"My behavior was completely out of line."

"We each had our own way of dealing with our family life when we were growing up." Jess rubbed her hand over her breastbone and then looked him straight in the eye. "Yours was to act out as crazy as you could to grab attention. Mine was to be as good as possible so I got to stay."

"So that's why you were always Little Miss Perfect?"

Jess snorted. "I was far from perfect but if you want to think that go right ahead." There was an easiness to her smile that had never been there before when they talked.

Con raised his brows. He'd never quite thought about each of them that way, but damn if she wasn't right. "Huh. When did you get to be so smart?"

"I was always smart," she countered. "You were just too busy being bad to see it."

"Well, I'm glad you figured it all out." Con bent

forward, thinking about that whole incident in a different light. It had been a pivotal moment in his life. He'd enlisted the next day determined to get out of Monterey before he destroyed everything.

"We good?" she asked softly.

A happy warmth settled in his heart. "Yeah. We're good."

Con decided it was time to move on to the business. "Well, one problem is solved."

"Hey. I resent being a problem." Jess smiled. "Kidding. What?"

"Jack called." Con frowned.

"Then why are you frowning?" Jess scooted until she was upright in the chair.

"There was definitely a woman in the background when he called," Con said. "And she sounded pissed."

Jess laughed. "And that's a problem? That sounds more like SOP for women and Jack."

"I can't put my finger on what was different." Con rubbed a hand over his smile. "It just was."

"At least he checked in," Jess replied.

"Yeah." Connor let that worry float away. They still had another bigger issue.

Jess asked the question that was on both their minds. "What about Riley?"

"Still no word. But hopefully he'll call in the next hour." Con said, "But if not, we need to be ready to go."

"Who made you in charge?" Jess tilted her head, but her words weren't confrontational just questioning.

"Jack."

"Okay then."

And that's when he really knew, everything was going to be all right. They discussed logistics and worries about Riley.

There was no sense worrying too much until he missed another check-in. But at least they had a game plan now.

Con had spent the last ten minutes trying not to surreptitiously check on Ava.

"Let me go check on the pictures." Jess stood.

"We really need to compare our notes regarding Fernandez." Con would rather not right now, but they had to make sure Fernandez was going down. The need to talk to Ava to make sure she knew exactly how he felt about her burned beneath his surface calm. "I need to make sure that the company is protected."

Jack had absolved him from the negative press of the almost arrest, and Con had protected the woman he loved and gotten some answers. Fernandez was definitely dirty. They just had to keep digging.

"What about Ava?" Jess said reluctantly. "She's more important than the company."

"No question," Con countered. "But it doesn't have to be an either/or situation. We can protect both Ava and the family."

"We can do it together," Jess said softly. "I'll give you a few minutes. I have a feeling you've got some more groveling to do." She glanced back at the reception area where Ava had been silent.

Shit. She'd probably had time to start thinking too much.

"Uh, yeah." Con thought about his declaration in Fernandez's office. Ava hadn't said much after that little caveman claim.

"Good luck. Don't be above begging." Jess bent over and pressed a kiss to his hair. She shot an amused glance at the desk and then sauntered away. "Just a reminder, this office worked great for me."

Once Jess was gone, Con called out. "Ava." He felt lighter, happier. Everything was going to work out.

Ava hovered in the doorway her hands clasped in front of her. But she was back to not meeting his gaze. Dammit.

Looks like he wasn't quite there yet. If he didn't distract her, she was going to bolt. Too much had changed in the last twenty-four hours and he didn't want to let her get away.

SUDDENLY BEYOND NERVOUS, Ava kept her gaze firmly planted on the crashing waves out the window rather than look directly at Con.

"Remind me never to piss you off, honey," Con teased.

Ava flushed about as deeply as she had when Jack had cautioned them not to have sex on his desk.

"So, *para* whatever. What does it mean?" Con stood and stretched. He'd taken off his suit jacket and his shirt pulled from the waist of his pants giving her a peep show of his abs.

Ava frowned and rubbed her hands along her arms. "It is not wise to open old wounds."

"Oh yeah. You got to him." A wide grin spread over his face and brightened his eyes. "You kicked butt."

A sense of pride rushed through her. She *had* kicked butt.

He sauntered toward her. She continued to linger in the doorway as if somehow when she stepped over the threshold things would never be the same.

"Now that the police have the entire incident documented and Fernandez knows that you have the Stone family as allies, you should be safe." Connor paused in front of her and brushed his fingers over her hair. "Or as safe as you can be until Fernandez is in jail."

"I hope we nail him," Ava said fiercely. She might not have been convinced before they went to see him but his reaction to their confrontation earlier told her he was definitely hiding something.

"We will." Con emphasized *we* reminding Ava of the other things revealed during that meeting.

Ava shied away from the memory of Con's claim. She was sure that he hadn't really meant it. He took things to heart deeply. And he had made it clear before they'd gone in that he would protect her. But that didn't mean he really wanted *her*.

Ava needed to get away. Needed time to process the events of the last thirty-six hours. "Can you take me home now that you and Jess are done?" Her car was still at the Stone mansion.

"We're not done. But not a chance." Connor denied her. As if to keep her from bolting, he curled his fingers around her left hand and held tight. "Right now, Fernandez can't move against you without bringing more scrutiny on himself, but he is still ridiculously clean on paper."

"I should be safe," Ava argued. If she didn't go home where was she going to go?

Connor shook his head, his gaze shadowed. "As we believed, he is deep into whatever happened to your friends. The fact that he could stay so clean for fifteen years means he's got the power and the ability to cover his tracks."

"But—"

"I requested an APB on the Lincoln. That pale green color is unusual enough that we might get a hit but it was likely stolen." Connor held her palm in his and rubbed his thumb over her soft skin.

"Okay."

"You have the softest skin." Con stroked his callused fingers over her palm.

"Yeah, well when you work in the fields you get really tough skin," Ava said absently. "I use about a gallon of moisturizer to keep my hands soft."

She was stuck back on not being able to go home. To get some distance from this overwhelming pull that Connor Stone seemed to exert on her. She glanced around the office and couldn't figure out for the life of her why he wanted her here. "What am I doing here?"

"Hey." Connor lifted her chin with his fingers and stared into her eyes. His tawny starburst gaze was hypnotic. "I see you."

"Of course you do, you're right in front of me."

Connor threaded his fingers through her hair. "I know why you want to leave."

"Umm, yes. Because I want to go home."

"No." Connor held her head tightly. His grip firm but not painful. "Because you have a giant hole inside you, a lonely gaping place that has existed since your friends disappeared."

She blinked. Swallowed.

"And now, this thing between us is filling that hole. Closing the gap and making you feel whole, making you *feel*, and you don't know how to deal with it."

Ava opened her mouth to argue but could only shake her head.

"The guilt is disintegrating and the idea that you might be able to live your life, be happy is suddenly a possibility. It's scary. I get that. I understand how you feel because I had that same hole inside me. But I realized that for the past year you've been slowly making me whole.

With each smile and averted gaze you've been filling those gaps."

"Connor." But she had no idea what to say. He was right. That hole had been there so long she wasn't even sure what to do. But now she was so full that she nearly choked on the emotions and feelings that wanted to burst from the overflowing pool.

She opened her mouth again but couldn't get anything out. She made him feel too?

Connor muttered. "Shit. Deeds not words."

What? Before she could ask, he yanked her over the threshold and pulled her into his arms. Con lifted her up and twirled her around. She couldn't believe he could lift her. "Connor! Put me down."

He laughed and let her slide down his body, the hard muscles of his chest rubbed against her breasts as she slid down to the floor. He cupped her jaw in his large palm, his hand tender yet forceful. "I love you."

What? His declaration left her speechless. Before she could reply to any of what he'd said in the last two minutes, Connor slanted his mouth across hers and devoured her with his kiss.

Tingles shivered down her spine, and her body heated at the sensual command in his kiss. Like a white knight who plundered his spoils, he invaded her mouth and explored her with his tongue. He nipped at her lips and scraped his teeth along her jaw. Then he pressed soft sucking kisses down her neck and along her delicate collarbone. As if she'd been tinder just waiting for his spark, her body ignited.

He kissed her as if he would never let her go. As if she filled him with the same contentment and desire that he gave to her.

He kissed her as if...he loved her. Connor Stone loved her.

She wanted to run. But then she thought about her vow to seize life. She could run or she could stay. Seize life. Seize Connor.

And she knew this was good, right. Ava blinked and swept her lashes over her eyes to hide the swell of love that shuddered through her. Her heart thundered in her chest at the step she was about to take. Fear and anticipation warred for dominance. But this was life. It was big and scary and wonderful. "I love you too."

Ava gripped his head and crashed his mouth to hers desperate for the hard press of his lips. Connor walked her further into the office until his butt hit the edge of Jack's desk. He pulled her tight into the V of his thighs and she was pressed up against him, her body snug between his legs. The proof of his desire throbbed against her belly and her arms were wrapped tight around his shoulders. Ava moaned into his mouth.

"Ready to de-brief. Oops!" Jess asked with laughter in her voice, "You want me to come back later?"

Ava tried to jump back like a teenager caught by her parents, but Connor held her tight. Her chest heaved and she knew her face was bright, candy apple red. *Madre de Dios.*

"Jesus, Jessica." Connor curled his arms around Ava's body and tucked her head into his shoulder. She didn't know if he were trying to protect her or himself since his erection prodded her belly insistently.

"I can go away for a few minutes." Jess Stone said, "You two look awfully comfortable on that desk."

Con lowered his head to Ava's shoulder but she could feel his smile against her neck. "Yeah."

Ava curled her arms around Connor and held on. She

and Con were practically sitting on Jack's desk with Ava between Connor's knees and it was likely clear they'd been about to take things further.

"I'm glad." Jess snickered. "That desk is certainly getting a workout."

"Yeah." Con acknowledged. "Jack should have never given us ideas."

"He's going to have to have his desk bronzed." Jess laughed again.

Ava buried her face against Connor's neck. "Oh my God."

"Don't worry, Ava." Jess said, "I'm partial to that desk too."

*Two weeks earlier*

Riley Stone didn't have a *type.*

He loved all women equally. Short, Tall, Skinny, Round. Outgoing. Shy. Young. Old. Sweet. Sexy. Surly.

And they loved him right back.

When he was younger, he'd come to the very happy conclusion, that he could charm his way out of, or sometimes into, any touchy situation.

He'd developed the skill as a young kid. When he'd realized that he was never going to be a good reader, or a good student, he'd made the decision that he'd have to rely on his other attributes. He could charm his grades up from any teacher in whose class he might need a little help. Which came in handy when he knew he wasn't going to pass a test.

He made it a point to always have something nice to say. As an adult, charming people was second nature. He didn't even have to think about doing it.

When he grew up, he finally understood that his talent was in making people feel better about themselves and better in general. How he approached a situation might vary from person to person, but if using a little charm eased the way, he was gonna use it.

He was shallow enough to use his God given talent to charm women into bed, at least he had been. These days he was more focused on making a go of GHR and Stone Consulting with his brothers and sister than in scoring with a hot woman.

But he still couldn't help himself when it came to charming people, especially women.

"How's it going, sweetheart?" He stopped to chat with Ava Sanchez, his brother Jack's assistant, making her blush and stammer. She was a complete hottie and didn't even seem to realize it. But Riley's Rules Number Ten: Never do more than lightly flirt with co-workers.

He'd managed to maintain an amicable relationship with every woman he'd ever had a thing with. It was a point of pride with him. But odds were, at some time, things wouldn't end well. And he'd never jeopardize a working relationship, or Global Humanitarian Relief and Stone Consulting, which meant sweet Ava was off limits.

He smiled gently at her. "He ready for me?"

"Yes. You can go on in," she replied with a tilt of her head. "He's got company."

"Client?"

She nodded, lowered her lashes and smiled.

"Okay." Riley paused to adjust the cuffs of his Egyptian cotton dress shirt and smooth his hand down his bright, geometric Jhane Barnes tie. He made it a point to be well-dressed in the office in case there were meetings with clients. It was rare but it did happen. From his vantage point in the doorway, he could see the woman in Jack's office. He didn't recognize her from the back. She seemed delicate, the curve of her head covered with a riot of short blond curls but her body language screamed supreme annoyance.

Riley curved his lips into a casual smile and sauntered into Jack's office. His big gruff brother seemed to be conversing carefully with the woman across from him.

Jack looked up and the hard set of his shoulders relaxed. "Ry, you're here." A desperate smile lit his face as he stood and grabbed Riley's hand like a lifeline. "I'd like you to meet, Diana Lundberg from *Tools for Schools*."

The woman stood abruptly and shoved out her hand in a very masculine move to greet him.

She was tall, more sleek lines and hard angles than soft curves but when her hard, capable fingers curled around his much larger palm, Riley took a serious punch to the gut. Lust hit, hard and unexpected, as he grasped her far more delicate fingers and gazed into her wary, pale blue eyes.

"Pleasure," he finally murmured dazedly.

She tugged her hand from his and turned to Jack. "*He's* going to take TFS into the jungle?" Her curved brow was derisive, and her tone bordered on insolent.

Jack leapt to Riley's defense. "He's extremely well-trained and has knowledge of the area."

"I'm a lot more adaptable than I look." Riley smiled seductively, unable to stop the flow of innuendo. He wanted her. Bad. He carefully put his hands in his pockets to stop the instinctive need to reach out and grab her hand again. He hated to do it as it ruined the line of his fine wool gabardine trousers but desperate times and desperate measures needed to be taken. It wouldn't do to accost the client.

She snorted. "I'm sure."

Her abrasive attitude was starting to drill into the haze

of attraction he had running through him. "Where am I headed?"

"Philippines," Jack clipped out. "Sulu, specifically."

Great. He'd had plenty of experience in country. Not his favorite as the political climate sucked almost as bad as the weather this time of year. Monsoon season was just about over, but the weather didn't always conform to the timetables put out by man. Not to mention the bugs. He shuddered. But he would deal. "Cargo?"

"School supplies," Jack replied.

"Piece of cake." Riley grinned, exposed his white teeth and tried to put her at ease. But he got lost in the magnetism she exuded like a force field even as he noted peripherally the angry vibe that radiated from her.

But angry babe wasn't put at ease. If anything, she stiffened even further, as her pale eyes shot sparks at him. "*I* am going to the Philippines. I am not so sure about you."

But Riley had stopped listening at *I*.

"Wait, what?" His eyebrows rose and he snapped his head toward Jack. He straightened from his nonchalant slouch and snatched his hands from his pockets. "You can't possibly expect me to take her," he gestured, careful to keep his voice low-key and well-modulated. "To Sulu Island."

A rosy flush of annoyance spread across her high delicate cheekbones as she pursed her pale pink lips and her body vibrated with a fine tension.

"Exactly," Di said. She dismissed Riley with a disdainful sweep of her lashes and trained her gaze on Jack. "Who else do you have?"

THANK you for reading Carved in Stone. I hope you enjoyed Connor and Ava's story!

Why didn't Riley and Di check-in? One click Heart of Stone (Riley, Family Stone #3) to find out!

Where is Jack? And do they finally catch Jose Fernandez? One click Still the One (Jack, Family Stone #4) to read more!

***

If you did enjoy this book, below are a few ways you can help a writer out!!

Good: Lend the book to a friend

Better: Recommend the book to your friends

Best: Leave a review at Amazon, BN, Goodreads, Apple Books, Kobo…basically any place they sell eBooks. Every review helps my work get out to other readers and I cannot even express how much it means to me when you let people know you liked my work. Readers have so many choices nowadays and limited dollars to spend. It can be difficult to take a chance on a new author even if the premise sounds appealing. By reviewing books, you give other readers insight into the story world and help them make informed purchases.

Thank you, thank you, thank you for your support!!

Where the Family Stone saga started….

In the early evening dusk, Jess Stone lay on her stomach in the twenty foot high rubble of a demolished church, underneath a black and gray city-scape tarp intended to camouflage her position. A sharp-edged chunk of debris dug into her lower rib cage, the scope of the Remington M24 cool and familiar against her face.

Her standard uniform of jeans, running shoes, and plain black t-shirt rendered her just another anonymous and transient relief worker...which she was actually. A black baseball cap hid her distinctive multi-hued blonde hair. The paper mask kept out the contaminated dust from the destroyed buildings but did little to stem the overwhelming stench of decaying bodies.

Tanks rumbled through the destroyed coastal town, their public address system blasting warnings for citizens to stay in their homes, curfew was in effect. The threat was a joke. Ninety percent of the people in the town didn't have homes left. Those who did were terrified to go back inside. In the fetid, humidity choked air, the tent cities erected in the parks and on the beach were seething masses of the injured and shock struck.

The substandard construction in the small country had never been enough to withstand the angry might of Mother Nature. Buildings had toppled like a stack of Tinkertoys, and left crumbling cement walls with twisted rebar poking out of the jagged ruins like a skeletal hand.

Trapped in the concrete pieces that littered the ground, the heat from the tropical day seared through her thin sturdy clothing. The stank of the raw sewage that ran in rivulets through the streets overpowered the salt-laden breeze off the ocean. People, covered with the grit of pulverized buildings and humans, shuffled along with blank vacant stares. Two weeks after the quake, still in shock, their lives decimated first by nature and then kicked and beaten by the ineffectiveness of a flawed relief system. Hundreds of humanitarian agencies had descended on the population duplicating efforts and yet completely missing the need in other areas. The government was ostensibly trying to coordinate the effort, however the mass chaos was undeniable.

Through the Leupold Ultra M3 fixed power sight, she tracked the movements of Henri LeRoy, leader of this tiny island nation, violator of human rights and dignity, and all around poor excuse for a human being.

Sickness roiled in her stomach. The power bar she'd eaten for breakfast threatened to add to the rubble pile as she tried to figure out how in the hell she'd ended up here. Back behind a sniper rifle with the power over life and death trembling in the muscles of her right trigger finger.

Dammit. When she'd decided to take control of her life and quit the FBI, she hadn't wanted to do this any more.

She'd wanted to be a simple relief worker. She'd wanted to connect with her family, brothers and mother.

But that bitch, fate, had slapped her upside the head and now here she was, where she'd sworn she never wanted to be again. Looking through the scope of a high-powered rifle, with a crystal clear head shot and a murky sense of right and wrong.

With little fanfare, she could blast LeRoy's brain matter all over the silk-covered walls and the antique Louis the XIV scrolled chairs in the receiving room of his ridiculously elegant weekend mansion which, since built properly, had sustained minimal damage. Her muscles twitched with the knowledge and acceptance that with one slow slide of her finger, the despotic, amoral leader would be history.

Jess didn't want to kill him, didn't want to be directly responsible for another death. She didn't want this choice. She'd given up this kind of life. She'd left the FBI after a series of high stress cases to get away from the doubt and guilt that had crippled her. To make her own decisions about right and wrong rather than carry out the commands of her bosses.

But if Henri LeRoy lived, chances were astronomical that many other citizens would die.

And yeah, she'd probably been manipulated into this. Actually no probably about it. Assassination had not been listed as one of her duties when she'd joined Global Humanitarian Relief. Damn her brother anyway.

But now all she could do was lay here in the desecrated remains of the former church and hope that her special skill set wouldn't be needed.

Fortunately, she was secondary backup.

And unless several things went horribly wrong, she would break down her weapon, get back to the relief aid encampment, back to actually helping people, and be out of here without ever firing her rifle.

Then she could hand out seed packets to her heart's content and figure out what she was going to do next. If she'd stay with GHR and her brothers, or go. First, she had to get through the next two hours.

But if something did go wrong...she prayed that if she was called upon, she could make the right decision. Make the shot. Cold zero.

Human trafficking is the number one global crime. There are trafficked women and children everywhere, even potentially in your own town. If you see somethings suspicious you can report it here: https://www.dhs.gov/blue-campaign/identify-victim

While S.S.A.F.E. is fictitious charity, there are several that help trafficked women. One excellent organization is Thistle Farms www.thistlefarms.org

# ALSO BY LISA HUGHEY

Black Cipher Files Romantic Suspense

The Encounter, A Prequel to Blowback

Blowback

Betrayals

Burned

Dangerous Game

**These books are also available in paperback

Black Cipher Files Box Set (includes Blowback, Betrayals, and Burned)

Snow Creek Christmas

Love on Main Street: A Snow Creek Christmas – 7 Author anthology

One Silent Night (from Love on Main Street)

Miracle on Main Street (standalone novella)

Family Stone Romantic Suspense

Stone Cold Heart, (Jess, Family Stone #1)

Carved in Stone (Connor, Family Stone #2)

Heart of Stone (Riley, Family Stone #3)

Still the One (Jack, Family Stone #4)

Jar of Hearts (Keisha & Shane, Family Stone #5)

Queen of Hearts (Shelley, Family Stone #6)

<u>Cold as Stone (John, Family Stone #7)</u>

<u>Family Stone Box Set (Stone Cold Heart, Carved in Stone, Heart of Stone, Still the One, & Jar of Hearts)</u>

<u>The Nostradamus Prophecies</u>

<u>View To A Kill #1</u>

Never Say Never #2

<u>ALIAS</u>

Stalked (ALIAS #1)

Hunted (ALIAS #2)

Vanished (ALIAS #3)

Deceived (ALIAS #4)

<u>Billionaire Breakfast Club</u>

His Semi-Charmed Life (Camp Firefly Falls #11 and Billionaire Breakfast Club #0)

Everything He Wants (Billionaire Breakfast Club #1 The Jock)

Queen of His Daydreams (Camp Firefly Falls #23 and Billionaire Breakfast Club #1.5)

**Stone Cold Heart:**

Jess Stone, former FBI sniper, always felt like the kid who looked in the candy store window but could never afford to go in. But on a humanitarian mission to aid an earthquake ravaged country, finally she finds a place where she fits, in Colin Davies' arms, and working for Global Humanitarian Relief, her big brother's company. But can the former SAS thaw Jess's stone cold heart?

**Carved in Stone:**

Connor Stone has always been odd man out in his family. Not the oldest, not the most charming, he'd had a lock on the youngest until another half-sibling came to live with them, so he raised hell in his youth. Con knows now the only way to redeem himself is with deeds, not words and sets out to prove once and for all he is worthy of the Stone family. When his older brother asks him to take care of business, Con finally will have redemption he craves. Except when Ava Sanchez, his brother's assistant, is threatened, he must choose between saving the girl or protecting his family. Will his choice bring him love or break his heart?

**Heart of Stone**:

Riley Stone is the handsome brother, the charming one. Everyone who meets him compares him to his father, which in his mind is not a compliment. But he's never met a woman he couldn't charm, until he meets Di, an acerbic, smart-mouthed, passionate activist who has no time for him or his charm. On the run, in the midst of danger, the blistering passion they share explodes. Can these two opposites find common ground, or will Di smash Riley's stone heart?

**Still the One:**

Jack Stone, former Navy SEAL, and oldest Stone sibling is determined to keep his family strong. Family is everything. So he starts Global Humanitarian Relief and Stone Consulting to do some good and keep his family together. But when he has to team up with his old flame, Bliss, on a missing persons case, an evil threatens him, his family and the one woman he could never forget and doesn't want to let go. Can these two former lovers put aside past hurts and heal their hearts?

**Jar of Hearts**:

Prickly Keisha Johnson has the hots for Shane Washington. But she's not about to reveal her inner soft heart to the player pilot and open herself up to hurt, until a favor to their boss sends them undercover and under the covers. Can she trust his sensual attention or will he shatter her fragile heart?

**Queen of Hearts**:

Ric Santana is in Las Vegas for his friend's wedding and some much needed R & R. But the vacation turns awkward when he discovers his smoking hot one night stand is actually his pal's stepmother. When Shelley's life is threatened, Ric doesn't hesitate to step into the role of bodyguard and protector. But as Ric grows closer to Shelley, he can't help but wonder, can he save her life or will they be too late for love?

**Cold As Stone**:

Nothing is ever set in STONE...

Retired Marine, John Pulaski, the surprise half-brother of the Stone siblings takes a trial job at Stone Consulting with hopes of making it permanent. Given a mission to find two missing women, John will stop at nothing to uncover the secrets to their abduction. His stunning and driven partner is the only hitch in his plan.

After a tragic incident two years ago, former FBI agent, Rissa Evans freezes at any sign of conflict, but she's bound and determined to overcome her personal obstacles to prove to her irresistibly sexy and infuriating partner that she's got what it takes to solve the case. As John and Rissa dig deeper into the case, their unwanted attraction intensifies, taking them both by surprise.

But the two wounded souls have to put aside their desires, in order to find the monster who steals the lives of innocent women. With time running out and so much on the line, can they let go of the scars of their past to discover what they're really looking for?

This book also includes Jack and Bliss's wedding. :)

# ACKNOWLEDGMENTS

No writer works in a vacuum. I am very fortunate to have a supportive group of writers and professionals behind me.

Huge thanks to Adrienne Bell, LGC Smith, and Cecilia Gray for pretty much everything and anything. A special shout out to Adrienne Bell for the ongoing word wars!! The Pens for being totally awesome-sauce, whether it be emergency pick-me-ups, or writing retreats at the haunted house, or impromptu sessions at Panera, or lunches at Buffalo Hot Wings.

To LJ at Mayhem Cover Creations. Thank you, thank you for the beautiful covers!

Thank you all. :)

# ABOUT LISA

USA Today Bestselling Author Lisa Hughey started writing romance in the fourth grade. That particular story involved a prince and an engagement. Now, she writes about strong heroines who are perfectly capable of rescuing themselves and the heroes who love both their strength and their vulnerability. She pens romances of all types—suspense, paranormal, and contemporary—but at their heart, all her books celebrate the power of love.

She lives in Cape Ann Massachusetts with her fabulously supportive husband, two out of three awesome mostly-grown kids, and one somewhat grumpy cat.

Beach walks, hiking, and traveling are her favorite ways to pass the time when she isn't plotting new ways to get her characters to fall in love.

Lisa loves to hear from readers and has tons of places you can connect with her. It's a wonder she gets any writing done at all....

Sign Up for Lisa's Confidants
Visit Lisa on the Web

[Follow Lisa's Boards on Pinterest](#)
[Follow Lisa on Instagram](#)
[Email Lisa](#)
[Be Lisa's Friend on Goodreads](#)
[Like Lisa on Facebook at Lisa Hughey: My Books](#)